NEVER A PROPER LADY

SECRETS OF SCANDALOUS LADIES
BOOK FIVE

COLLETTE CAMERON

For permission requests, write to the publisher at the address below.
Attn: Permissions Coordinator
info@collettecameronbooks.com
collettecameronbooks.com
eBook ISBN: 978-1-955259-23-1
Print Book ISBN: 978-1-966087-33-5

FREE BOOK!

JOIN MY EXCLUSIVE MAILING LIST
Collette Cameron Newsletter

AND GET A FREE EBOOK!

https://collettecameronbooks.com/freegift

Plus Sneak Peeks, Giveaways, Contests, Exclusive Content, and More... P.S. I promise only good stuff ~ **no** spam!

and in fact, becomes immensely digestible reading!" ~ *VA Joanie*

★★★★★ "I loved these two as individuals. I loved them as a couple. With the secondary characters in full swing and making their ways through the story, this was a magnificent read." ~ *Kristi Hudecek-Ashwill*

DEDICATION

For every reader who wants to read just one more page...

ONE

Naturally, I shall attend Lottie's wedding, but I cannot promise to remain for the house party's duration. You know how much I detest the boorish things, Edie. Particularly as I know our odious Kellinggrave cousins will be present.

Besides, my research won't permit me to fritter away an entire week on frivolous activities. Toward that end, my amanuensis, my valet, and perhaps even my research assistant shall accompany me to Dovetonwick Court.

Please inform Mother and ask her to make the arrangements. Also, give her, Lottie, and the rest my warmest regards. Expect us Thursday next.

~Lord Constantine Kellinggrave, in response to his sister, Lady Edyth Kellinggrave's reminder of their sister's upcoming nuptials

29 August 1818

Bedford Square, London, England
A few minutes past seven in the morning

Shirtsleeves rolled to his elbows and sans jacket and waistcoat, Constantine—Con to his closest friends and family—stood before his scuffed and scarred double-sided walnut partner desk. Eyes narrowed, he cocked his head, listening.

Yes, the brisk footsteps he'd come to recognize these past few days announced his amanuensis had arrived for work. Early again, as she had been every day since he'd grudgingly retained her services.

Regrettably, he couldn't fault her for her promptness.

Time to don his armor, gird his loins, gather his shield and sword, and prepare for battle.

He swept a gaze around the room, which had become less research sanctuary and more combat zone in recent days.

Soft rays of sunshine filtered through the open navy-blue draperies festooning the three arched windows opposite the long room. The streams of sunlight caressed the equally scuffed and scarred oak floor and the single taupe, crimson, and cerulean-blue Aubusson carpet sprawled haphazardly in the center of the rectangular room.

Dust motes floated in the luminous beams, performing a taunting dance before they drifted to rest on the myriad of surfaces cluttered with specimens, journals, documents, and all manner of curiosities. And dust. A fine layer coated almost everything.

Gilly, the once emaciated mongrel of undeterminable pedigree Constantine had rescued from the streets two years ago, lay prone upon the floor, soaking in those same rays. As if sensing his master's focus, Gilly thumped his wiry, multi-colored tail once without deigning to open his copper-brown eyes.

A wry grin pulled Constantine's mouth upward on one side.

Gilly had taken to a life of luxury and ease as readily as a nobly born duke.

The feminine stride grew closer and, if possible, even sharper, as if the deceptively decorous Miss Faith Roth announced with her dainty feet what she didn't dare say with her pink Cupid's bow mouth.

Not that he initially noticed her pretty mouth.

It's just that she so often pursed those plump lips, pulled them into a disapproving ribbon, or bit the lower pillow—no doubt to prevent telling him to bugger himself—that he couldn't help but notice how nicely shaped they were.

Never mind Miss Roth's lips.

Another day of subtle verbal sparring and intellectual dueling was about to commence.

You enjoy matching wits with her.

Constantine snorted, and Gilly cracked open a sleepy eye.

Determining naught was amiss, the dog relaxed and resumed his nap with a shuddery sigh.

Not by half, Constantine didn't enjoy the daily scuffles with his scribe. No more than he'd relish a carbuncle on his bum or appreciate a monstrous stye in his eye.

Refusing to look toward the entrance, yet acutely aware of each clipped step drawing Miss Faith Roth nearer, he drew his eyebrows together as he considered the scientific journals he held in either hand.

Would he have time to read either or both while traveling to Dovetonwick Court for his sister's wedding? Likely. With a nonchalant shrug, he added the books to the stack of papers, books, and documents he'd already placed inside his satchel.

Naturally, not attending the nuptials wasn't an option—

Mother would never forgive Constantine—and he wanted to see Lottie exchange her vows.

Regardless, this was a deuced inconvenient time to leave his research.

In truth, there was never a good time for a man who preferred scientific studies to socializing with vain, self-important denizens. Many of whom looked down their aristocratic noses at his *hobby*. But as the third son of Harland Kellinggrave, Duke of Landrith, they daren't overtly disdain Constantine or the work he took seriously.

Pompous hypocrites.

Moreover, a fortnight ago, his faithful and reliable research assistant, Harvey Camberg-Trainer, had fallen in love with the pretty clerk at the new French patisserie and boulangerie. Now Harvey was distracted more often than not and had actually confused a Holly Blue butterfly with a common blue just yesterday.

Harvey's doleful countenance and soul-rending sighs every few minutes as he rested his chin upon his fist and gazed forlornly out the window were enough to cause Constantine to clench his teeth and swear beneath his breath.

Must love render men bacon-brained sots?

Buffleheaded idiots?

Constantine had never suffered from the affliction—praise the saints—but two of his closest chums had. Half the time, he scarcely recognized the perpetually grinning dolts anymore.

If Harvey brought another bag of pastries or loaf of bread to work, Mrs. Mettlebank might well give her notice. The cook didn't appreciate another outshining her culinary talents. Even Constantine had to admit the French baked goods were superior to anything Mrs. Mettlebank had ever served.

He'd bite his tongue off before admitting that fact, however.

Mrs. Mettlebank accepted his idiosyncrasies, including that he rarely dined on any type of schedule. And she didn't grumble about him wandering into the kitchen at all hours for a snack. More often than not, she left a plate of something or other for him to sample.

More irksome than Harvey's infatuation, however, was Faith Roth, the scrivener Constantine had recently hired. And who, any second now, would march into the laboratory-office and, with a single astute glance from those chocolatey doe eyes behind her wire-rimmed spectacles, under sardonically arched strawberry blonde eyebrows, would prick his temper.

As surely and as deliberately as if she'd poked him with a needle.

Had a more exasperating woman ever walked the earth?

She seemed particularly fond of sending verbal darts in his direction, always with a benign expression and perfectly respectable tone.

Miss Faith Roth didn't fool him for a second.

Beneath her cool and calm exterior bubbled molten lava. Unless he missed his guess—and he was positive he did not—she'd erupt someday, and anyone nearby would get scorched.

Despite her outward poise and decorum, Miss Roth had become a proverbial thorn in Constantine's side. He'd yet to see her lose her temper, but her expressive eyes rung him a peal at least half a dozen times daily.

He couldn't terminate her either because not only was she efficient, organized, and an excellent scribe—which Constantine admitted he badly needed—he'd only hired her because he'd lost a bet.

A silly, thoughtless wager he never ought to have placed and wouldn't have done so if he hadn't had one brandy too many, and if Lord Ronan Brockman and Aston Terramier hadn't accused him of being archaic in his beliefs and resistant to social progress—specifically when it came to women.

Those two disgustingly in love chaps thought it hysterical that Constantine had hired Faith Roth, who just happened to be—God save him—bosom friends with their sweethearts.

Fate had an irregular sense of humor.

By Jove, Lord Constantine Peyton Harland Kellinggrave was *not* antiquated in his thinking.

Despite ridicule and condescension, wasn't he going beyond the bounds and researching the effects of butterflies and moths on pollination?

Pollination was crucial for crops, orchards, and even kitchen gardens. Bees generally received all of the attention, but moths and butterflies traveled greater distances and contributed mightily to pollination as well.

He tapped his chin with his forefinger.

Hmm. Were nectar-feeding bats also pollinators?

That might be interesting to study as well, but first things first.

Miss Faith Roth.

The perpetual pebble in his shoe. The burr on his bum. The itch he couldn't reach.

If Constantine gave his scrivener her *congé* before six months passed, he'd have to admit defeat and pay the wager. It wasn't losing the funds that made him reluctant. It was that he'd have to admit there might be a measure of truth—surely, only the merest amount—in his friends' accusation.

Why was a young woman of excellent character so set on proving herself in a traditionally male occupation? Not that females couldn't perform the task just as well, but the women he knew focused their energies on marriage and having children.

The gentlemanliness bred into Constantine's very core as

an aristocrat also objected to the dishonor of hiring her purely to win a wager. That had been the craven act of a cad, and he felt no small amount of shame for his role in the fiasco.

That Miss Roth had overheard him arguing with Harvey about why he'd hired her only added to Constantine's guilt. Now, every time Miss Roth glanced in his direction, he felt miniature accusatory daggers pricking him.

Grunting, he plunked his hands on his hips and perused his disorderly research laboratory and office once more. Which was, in fact, the entire ground floor of his house except for the kitchen.

How hard would it be to convince Miss Roth to accompany him to Dovetonwick Court? He had mentioned possible travel as part of her duties during the farcical interview, hoping the duty would dissuade her from accepting the post. It hadn't.

Confounded woman.

If Constantine dictated to her during the journey, that would make up for the time lost participating in obligatory family activities.

He wished to depart for Dovetonwick Court on Tuesday —three days away.

"Good morning, my lord."

Formal, cool, civil.

Constantine painted a pleasant expression on his face and summoned a welcoming smile.

"Good morning, Miss Roth. I trust you slept well."

He barely constrained the grin tipping his lips upward at her swift, suspicious glance. He'd never bothered to inquire about her sleep or any other personal details, for that matter, before.

Except for the perfunctory questions he'd asked during their initial meeting, he knew nothing about her. Beyond her name, age—three and twenty—education, that she was an orphan, and that her letters of reference were exceptional.

Of course, the latter could've been forged, but he believed them genuine.

Of the three women who'd answered his advert, Miss Roth was the candidate he'd erroneously believed would quit within a week.

More fool him.

Everything he'd done to encourage Miss Roth's departure had only caused her to dig her heels and claws in and thwart his efforts all the more. Always within the bounds of respectfulness and deference.

Only just.

Gilly leaped to his feet and trotted over to Miss Roth, wagging his tail with such exuberance that his entire back end wiggled.

Traitor.

"Good morning to you too, handsome boy," Miss Roth crooned, bending to give the dog a pat and kiss, and presenting her delightfully rounded derriere for leisurely inspection in the process.

By Zeus. Constantine was *not* jealous of a dog, and by no stretch of the imagination was Gilly a *handsome boy*. Not with that tattered ear that dropped over his forehead, nor his doggy smile that rather made him appear as if he'd indulged in too much ale.

Swiveling away, Constantine raked a hand through his hair, messing the already untidy strands further. He hadn't bothered with brushing it into one of the fashionable styles the young bucks of the *ton* favored.

Embly had long since given up on Constantine's unruly, overly long hair. Keeping him reasonably shaven and presentable in unrumpled attire strained the bounds of the valet's best intentions.

At least Embly hadn't threatened to give his notice *this* week.

That was an improvement.

Constantine slid the bane of his existence a side-eyed glance.

Miss Roth would smite him to cinders if she caught him gawping at her backside.

He did not ogle or dally with his female employees. Given Mrs. Mettlebank was five and sixty if she was a day and weighed three stone more than he did, and as Miss Roth scarcely contained her disdain of him, there wasn't any desire to ogle to begin with.

He added another scientific article to the satchel upon his desk.

As Miss Roth removed her bonnet, her gaze, which never missed a detail, landed on the bulging satchel.

"Are you going somewhere, my lord?"

Folding his arms, Constantine rested his hips against the edge of the desk.

"As a matter of fact, we are."

"*We?*" She paused in drawing off her plain straw bonnet. Her dark brown eyes rounded, and her attention shifted to the bag and then back to him. "I beg your pardon. I thought you said *we*."

He grinned, delighting in flummoxing her for once.

"I did indeed, Miss Roth." He nodded and crossed his ankles. "We. You, me, Embly, Mr. Camberg-Trainer, and Gilly depart for Dovetonwick Court at first light on Tuesday."

He hadn't informed Harvey yet, and his friend might refuse, given his current infatuation. Embly would suffice as a chaperon, he supposed.

Had you hired a male amanuensis, you would not need a chaperone.

Water under the bridge.

Constantine *had* hired a female, so he must deal with the consequences.

"I..." Miss Roth swallowed as she slowly lifted the hat from her head, revealing the mass of glorious fair curls threaded with bronze, gold, and fire ribbons. Her hair betrayed her, revealing the spitfire's temperament before she opened her mouth. "*This* Tuesday?"

"I did mention when I hired you that the position involved the possibility of travel."

He'd hoped that particular detail would put her off. Traveling unescorted with a male and all that. Any sensible miss would've gone pale and promptly bid him good day.

Miss Roth had not.

Constantine quirked an eyebrow, anticipating her response.

"Yes, you did, my lord."

Remarkably composed, she hung her bonnet on the coat rack, removed her gloves, and then her deep green spencer. Today, she wore a yellow calico gown sprinkled with pastel flowers.

She appeared young and pretty and feminine.

It was the first time he could recall that she hadn't worn a severe, drab-colored frock or masculine waistcoat and skirt. He presumed she preferred severe styles and unassuming colors. The modest but tasteful gown she wore today revealed again how little he knew or understood about Miss Roth.

Folding her hands before her, she tilted her head to the side. "This is a business trip?"

"Business and pleasure." Constantine scratched his chin,

the stubble beneath his fingers reminding him he ought to shave. It had been three—no, four—days.

"My eldest sister is getting married."

At one and thirty, three years Constantine's senior, Charlotte had waited for true love.

"I see." A spark of defiance glinted in Miss Roth's eyes, and she set her shoulders at a recalcitrant angle. "And if I decline to accompany you?"

Clasping his hands behind him, he twisted his mouth into a wry smile.

"Sadly, Miss Roth, I would deem it grounds for termination."

"*Sadly*? I'll just bet," she murmured so softly that Constantine barely heard her.

Was this the excuse he had been looking for?

His way to rid himself of the delightfully irritating Miss Roth?

Why wasn't he thrilled at the notion then?

Because who would transcribe for him? Take precise, excellent dictation in a neat script? Organize his sloppily written notes? Straighten and organize the debacle that was his office and laboratory?

"I see," she said again, a trifle louder. Inhaling a deep breath—likely to keep from telling Constantine precisely what she thought of him—she angled toward her tidy desk. "What time should I be here?"

"No need." Straightening, Constantine waved his hand. "I'll collect you at six. Leave your direction with my coachman." He studied her from beneath half-closed eyelids. The air fairly crackled with her disapproval.

He didn't know what devil on his shoulder prompted him, but he drove the point home. "It's a three-day journey. Each way."

Miss Roth sank gracefully onto her chair and began arranging her instruments. She picked up the notes he'd left for her and, forehead puckered, perused them.

"Three days in a coach. Bloody marvelous," she muttered beneath her breath, her lips scarcely moving. "Six if you count both ways."

Her one imperfection.

Miss Roth talked to herself.

More often than naught, she murmured something unflattering about his character.

"Did you say something, Miss Roth?"

Constantine couldn't quite check his satisfied grin.

She glanced up and fashioned an insincere smile. No hint of warmth shone in the frosty stare she leveled him.

Weren't brown eyes the color of treacle supposed to be warm?

Constantine was positive she wished him to the lowest level of Hades.

"Nothing of import, my lord."

Unable to restrain his humor any longer, he chuckled, and she skewered him with those big pansy eyes.

Picking up the quill, she held it suspended. "She who laughs last laughs longest."

Quoting Shakespeare, is she?

She was full of surprises today.

Miss Faith Roth was a perplexing enigma.

"Is that a challenge, Miss Roth?"

"Heavens, no, my lord." She bent her bright head to her task. "Consider it more of a prophecy."

TWO

Lord Constantine insists I accompany him to his familial estate. If I do not, he'll terminate my employment. I shall not give him the satisfaction and can only hope the contents of my stomach stay put. You know I don't travel well. I'm quite beside myself, anticipating the journey and possible humiliating consequences of an extended coach trip.

I can hardly carry a bucket or a chamber pot aboard and hover over it the entire journey. Pray for me. I shall need it!

Purity told me in her last letter that she saw Trinity Ablethorne at a house party. I wasn't aware Trinity had returned to England. I wish I had her constitution for traveling. I should very much like to see her.

~Miss Faith Roth, in a letter to her
girlhood friend, Chasity Noble

3 September 1818
Five miles from Dovetonwick Court
On a wretchedly bumpy stretch of road
A few minutes past three in the afternoon

Pressed into the coach's corner, Faith clamped her jaw and squeezed her eyes shut tighter. A miserable moan clawed up her throat, but she swallowed it.

I shall not vomit. I shall not vomit.

Amid the pounding between her ears, the bile burning her throat, and her waffy stomach, she was utterly and wholly miserable.

Three days of torment had culminated in this final leg of their journey on what had to be the worst track she'd ever had the misfortune of traveling. Even Lord Constantine Kellinggrave's well-sprung coach and thickly upholstered sage-green velvet seat couldn't prevent Faith's teeth from jarring and her bum from bouncing.

Embly, also suffering from motion sickness, had opted to ride atop with the coachmen.

That reprieve was not an option for Faith, or she'd have seized it.

Still, she had the gratification of once again thwarting Lord Constantine's obvious attempt to get her to resign.

A morose Harvey Camberg-Trainer sat opposite her beside a surprisingly solicitous Lord Constantine. Mr. Camberg-Trainer's lady love had another beau, and Mr. Camberg-Trainer had bemoaned fate and providence most of the journey from London.

His lordship had given up on his dictation efforts after the first hour when Faith finally confessed reading or writing while in a moving conveyance would likely cause her to cast up her crumpets on his glossy boots.

Not that she'd eaten crumpets or anything else for that matter. She hadn't dared much more than a thin soup and a few bites of bread the night before they departed and not much more than dry bread since.

Why did some people have no adverse effect to the jarring and bouncing, yet she was overcome with malaise? Probably the same reason why some people suffered greatly from sea sickness and the churning and pitching of the ocean didn't affect others at all.

Gilly occupied the seat beside her, his shaggy head in her lap. The dog had attempted to offer what doggy comfort he could between lengthy naps. He whimpered in his sleep, his legs twitching as he dashed after something in his dream.

She idly patted his back to soothe him while keeping the palm of her other hand firmly pressed to her roiling belly.

A wheel dropped into a pothole, and a stifled oath escaped his lordship.

Mr. Camberg-Trainer grunted as he scooted further back onto the seat.

"I say, Con. The roads in Essex leave something to be desired."

"Indeed," came his lordship's droll response. "More so each time I visit."

Another sharp dip resulted in a hissing breath escaping between Faith's teeth.

God save me.

How much more of this can I endure?

"We're almost there, Miss Roth," Lord Constantine advised, almost kindly.

So he'd reassured her the past ten miles.

Not daring to open her mouth to respond for fear of what might pour forth, Faith made an affirmative sound in her throat.

All she wanted was for the constant motion to stop and then to crawl into bed for a week. After a long soak in a tub of scented water, of course, to wash the travel grime from her person.

Realizing her dream of becoming a scrivener didn't seem very jolly at the moment. Nevertheless, the obstinate man across from her would not triumph. He had hinted many times he didn't think she was up to the task. By heavens, a little sick stomach and a wee headache would not provide him the victory he sought.

"I intend to commandeer my father's study while we are at Dovetonwick." Lord Constantine's melodic baritone interrupted the silence.

Faith opened her eyes, her gaze colliding with his lordship's bottle-green glance.

The duke might have different thoughts about his son and associates taking over his private space.

"It's the only place that won't be overrun with guests," Lord Constantine explained.

Which was precisely why the duke would likely kick up a fuss.

"Unless I can persuade Mother to let us use the dower house."

Had he considered the impropriety of such an arrangement?

But then again, there was nothing proper about a lord employing a female scrivener, and Faith had known that from the beginning. She'd chosen to follow her dream rather than submit to outdated and repressive social expectations.

Lord Constantine glanced out the window and rubbed his square chin. He wore no gloves, and, for the umpteenth time, Faith tried to decide if he cocked a snook at propriety or if he was oblivious to the oversight.

Likely, the latter.

"Yes, the dower house," he mused to himself. "That would be ideal. No guests poking about. More privacy and fewer interruptions."

Faith hadn't thought to ask what her role would be beyond a scrivener.

Would she be housed with the servants?

House parties tended to swell estates to bursting with guests bringing their essential servants, from valets and abigails to coachmen.

In truth, it was rather poor form for Lord Constantine to drag his assistant and scribe to a family affair—particularly something as illustrious as a wedding and an extended house party.

Faith would vow he'd not have nearly as much time to work on his research as he anticipated. Which begged the question, what was she to do with herself?

Well, if he wanted to pay her wages when she had little to do, that was his concern.

As if reading her mind, he swept his firm mouth into a mocking grin. "I assure you, my family is accustomed to me disappearing for hours on end for my research. You'll not be left to your own devices."

"More's the pity," Mr. Camberg-Trainer complained with a good-natured grin. "I'd hoped the duchess would keep you so engaged that I might have myself a holiday. I'm certain Miss Roth wouldn't mind a few days to recreate."

He winked at Faith, and she managed a weak smile.

Gilly stirred, stretched, and then passed wind.

"Good God above," Mr. Camberg-Trainer gasped as he struggled to lower the window.

"What did you feed the mongrel, Con?"

"Must've been the mutton," Lord Constantine

mumbled beneath the handkerchief clamped over his nostrils. His eyes danced with a combination of hilarity and apology.

Faith held her palm over her nose and encouraged the animal from the seat.

Given her unsettled stomach, enduring Gilly's digestive disorders might have her casting up her accounts after all. Grateful for the fresh air the lowered window provided, she drew a steadying breath and focused on the men.

Mr. Camberg-Trainer was the opposite of Lord Constantine in almost every way. Immaculately attired, small and wiry, dark-haired and eyed, he was kind, possessed a refreshing sense of humor, and didn't take himself too seriously.

He was also highly intelligent—one of the few traits he shared with his lordship.

"My lord, you never did explain how the third son of a duke came to be captivated by science."

Faith had never put the question to him directly before. She'd wondered, of course, but didn't feel it was her place to inquire.

Why she did so now baffled.

His mouth skewed to the side in what could only be called a droll smile, Lord Constantine rubbed his nose.

"What you are really asking, Miss Roth, is why didn't I go into the clergy like third sons are expected to do?"

A silly business that, in her opinion. Birth order didn't dictate where one's preferred interests should lay. Although, if she were perfectly candid, one's birth often determined the options available to a person.

Take Faith, for instance.

Raised at Haven House and Academy for the Enrichment of Young Women, she had few choices of employment, the most common being companion, governess, or school instructor.

In truth, she'd never actually expected to be hired as a scrivener.

She wasn't going to muck it up either, and if that meant biting her tongue to keep from telling the too handsome but somewhat absent-minded Lord Constantine Kellinggrave to go bugger himself, well, she'd sport a sore tongue.

"I did toddle down the respectable path of becoming a man of God for just over a year." His lordship rolled a shoulder. "I realized it was not my calling."

"I'll say it wasn't." Mr. Camberg-Trainer grinned unabashedly.

Well. Well.

There was a fascinating story there. Faith was positive.

His lordship silenced him with a darkling scowl that held no real censure. "I saw no point in pursuing something I could not commit to with all my heart. Fortunately, my parents agreed and allowed me to pursue other avenues."

The Duke and Duchess of Landrith sounded genuinely caring. They'd tolerated their eldest daughter waiting to marry for love when arranged marriages and marriages of convenience were *de rigueur*. They'd allowed their youngest son to pursue an unusual career when the aristocracy disdained any association with gainful employment.

"But why this particular branch of science? Lepidopterology?" A visit to Hatchard's on Piccadilly provided Faith with that useful tidbit. She'd assured herself that any amanuensis worth her salt would know her employer's profession, and that was the only reason she'd purchased a dusty tome on the subject.

When Lord Constantine didn't answer but instead observed her with those penetrating green eyes, as if he sought to see inside her head, Faith persisted. "The study of butterflies and moths?"

Anything to keep her mind off the nausea plaguing her.

Lord Constantine lifted a broad shoulder. "They fascinate me, and I believe I can use my research to benefit mankind. Why did you choose to become an amanuensis?"

Faith glanced out the window at the passing landscape. Black-faced sheep dotted the verdant fields, interrupted now and again by small groves of trees, mostly oak. A pair of red deer does warily watched the coach's progress from beneath the shelter of a pine tree.

"I suppose," she said, directing her regard back to his lord-ship, "because God put the desire there. Even when most people said it was impossible, I believed I could become a scrivener."

Most people?

Everyone. Even kind-hearted Hester Shepherd who'd raised Faith

"*'Tis simply not done, Faith. You would do better to accept that truth and turn your attention to a viable career path, my dear.*"

"Brava for you, Miss Roth," Mr. Camberg-Trainer chimed in. "Con's lucky to have you."

Faith was positive Lord Constantine didn't agree. *Yet.* However, she was determined to become indispensable to him.

A few minutes later, the coach finally jerked to a stop in the circular brick drive in front of a magnificent manor house. Meticulously trimmed shrubberies paralleled the drive, and two gargantuan stone urns on either side of the well-scrubbed stairs contained double spiral topiaries.

They also revealed the gardener's zealousness for perfection.

Everything about the house bespoke sophistication, wealth, and extravagance.

Faith had been educated and trained how to conduct herself in all circumstances. Nonetheless, she swallowed as she eyed the regal structure with its dozens of windows gleaming in the afternoon sun. If the ostentatious mansion contained fewer than two hundred rooms, she'd forgive Lord Constantine for putting her through the past three days of torture.

For the first time in a long while, uncertainty tapped at her conscience.

What kind of reception could she expect?

Well, there was nothing for it.

Faith was here because her employer—obstinate, privileged bounder—demanded she be. As an employee, she'd not be obligated to participate in house party activities, and she wouldn't be scrambling to accommodate the elite guests because she wasn't a household servant.

Why, she might even find time to catch up on her correspondence and read the novel by Jane Austen, *Northanger Abbey*, that she'd impulsively purchased that day at Hatchard's.

Not waiting for the coachman to open the door, Lord Constantine alighted. Mr. Camberg-Trainer followed, and he turned to assist Faith from the conveyance.

Gilly jumped down and promptly found a bush to relieve himself upon. Then with an exuberant bark, he dashed toward the stables. He obviously knew his way about the estate.

Having the oddest sensation that someone watched her, Faith scanned the closest windows. There, a curtain fluttered at a window above them. Most likely, a relative was excited that his lordship was home.

Lord Constantine turned to her, a furrow above the bridge of his nose.

"Miss Roth, I would be amiss if I..."

He paused, uncertainty and hesitation whisking across his sculpted features.

How peculiar.

Still feeling like ponies performed cartwheels in her stomach, Faith met his gaze. Something akin to worry or concern shadowed his verdant gaze under those sometimes-intimidating hawkish sandy eyebrows.

"My lord?"

The door swung open, revealing the majordomo. Eyes alight with merriment, the butler's wrinkled face crumpled into a smile.

"Welcome home, my lord."

"Thank you, Berkham. It's good to be here."

Three footmen in blue and gold livery descended the steps and set to unloading the luggage.

"Constantine! You're finally home!"

A pretty young blonde wearing a sunny jonquil gown trimmed in Pomona green ribbon and white lace sprinted down the stairs and threw her arms around him.

Likely the window watcher.

Expression amiable—almost doting—the butler looked on in approval from his position at the top of the stairs.

Chuckling, Lord Constantine lifted the girl as if she weighed no more than a kitten and twirled her around before setting her on the ground.

This must be his lordship's youngest sister. On the journey to Dovetonwick Court, he'd explained that her addition to the family when he was thirteen had come as quite a surprise. She'd displaced him as the baby of the family, for which he claimed he was heartily grateful.

"Edie." He gave her a playful wink. "I vow you've grown into a rare beauty."

"Pshaw. What flim-flam." Cheeks flushed, she grinned up at him. "You saw me not more than three months ago, Con."

Faith glanced at the house and puzzled her brow upon noticing sky-blue skirts in the opening behind the butler.

Another family member?

No, surely whoever she was, she'd have greeted Lord Constantine too.

An eavesdropping guest, then?

For what purpose?

Was the earwigger one of those women who thrived on bearing tales?

Clasping her brother's hand, Lady Edyth turned a friendly smile upon Faith. Curiosity sparkled in her eyes, a lighter shade of green than her brother's.

"You know Harvey Camberg-Trainer, Edyth," his lordship said.

"Lady Edyth Kellinggrave." Mr. Camberg-Trainer bowed. "A pleasure as always."

His lordship extended his hand toward Faith. "This is Miss Faith Roth, my amanuensis."

"A *woman*?" Lady Edyth Kellinggrave's eyes grew impossibly round, and her voice pitched upward. "Your amanuensis is a...woman?"

Still feeling the rolling motion of the coach and very much wanting to find a solid place to sit, Faith smiled. "Indeed."

"Oh, Mama shall have a fit of the vapors, Con."

Lady Edyth bit her lower lip, genuine apprehension furrowing her smooth brow. "She's already quite put upon and has been in a dither for days with all the arrangements for the wedding."

Lady Edyth looped her arm through her brother's elbow.

"And why is that, minx?" he asked, giving her an affectionate sideways grin.

"Mama thought your amanuensis was a man and put him —um, *her*—in the same chamber as Mr. Camberg-Trainer." She darted Faith an apologetic glance. "Which, of course, won't do at all. The house is full to the rafters. Or it will be by tomorrow. We've even moved our servants to the attics. There are simply *no* beds available."

"I'm sure it's not as dire as all that, Edie," Lord Constantine soothed.

Given Lady Edyth's expression, Faith would wager it *was* as dire all that.

Perfect.

She didn't have a bed to lie down on.

At this juncture, she'd take a pallet on the floor in a linen closet. She eyed the coach she'd just vacated. Or a seat inside a coach would suffice.

"Have our Kellinggrave cousins arrived yet?" Lord Constantine asked in a voice a trifle too nonchalant.

Edyth pulled a face. "No. They'll arrive tomorrow. Although Martin traveled directly from Kent and arrived a couple of hours ago."

"One day of reprieve, eh?" his lordship quipped.

Nodding, she slid Faith a glance, obviously wanting to say more but refraining in front of the others.

Ah, so the cousins weren't on the best of terms.

Lord Constantine abruptly changed the subject.

"Miss Roth can use my bedchamber."

The merest crease between his eyebrows, he gave Faith a searching glance. Could he see that she was about to topple over?

"I'll share with Harvey," he said. "No harm, no foul."

He offered a reassuring grin to the trio that gaped at him as if he'd sprung an elephant's trunk upon his aristocratic face.

Faith speared a swift glance to the doorway.

The eavesdropper had slipped away. She'd probably been the person peeking out the draperies earlier when Faith sensed someone watched her.

Who was she?

Had she heard Lord Constantine's suggestion?

The butler had, for certain.

Berkham blinked several times and opened and closed his mouth twice.

Had Lord Constantine lost his mind?

True, he was often absent-minded, and Faith had frequently observed that he discarded or ignored strictures, but to offer her his chamber?

Good Lord, the implications...

Faith shook her head, instantly regretting the motion when her skull threatened to tumble off her shoulders and roll down the drive. "I don't think—"

"At least for a lie-down, Miss Roth, until other arrangements can be made."

Lord Constantine's solicitous and conciliatory tone gave her pause.

She searched his face.

If Faith didn't know better, she'd suspect genuine concern motivated his lordship's generosity.

"She does not look at all well," he observed to his sister, and Faith wasn't certain whether surprise or offense stiffened her spine and squared her shoulders.

Approval shone in his eyes.

Why the bounder had done that on purpose. Deliberately provoked Faith into a defensive stance.

Lady Edyth eyed Faith, sympathy softening her pretty eyes. "She is rather pale, poor thing."

"I am standing right here," Faith put in, earning a hastily muffled chuckle from Mr. Camberg-Trainer.

Well, really.

Didn't they know it was impolite to discuss someone as if they were a flower blossom or a piece of fruit?

"Oh, forgive me. I meant no offense." Edyth released her brother's arm and took Faith's instead. "Let me show you up, Miss Roth. We'll leave Con to deal with Mama."

A masculine groan filled the air.

Was the duchess that formidable?

Faith opened her mouth to object again, but Lord Constantine shook his head.

"Have a lie-down, Miss Roth. Now is not the time for you to display your mulishness."

The bleating in her head had reached a crescendo, and Faith reluctantly allowed Lady Edyth to guide her inside.

She should never have come, but stubbornness had a way of provoking one into untenable situations.

My reputation shall be in shambles.

THREE

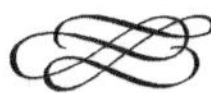

I shall be there Friday before noon. It's the earliest I can manage. I imagine I shall be the last to arrive, and I do apologize. But as you are aware, a soldier is seldom the master of his time.

Please do ask Cook to ensure plenty of ginger biscuits are on hand. Those served at Whitehall are as unpalatable as hardtack.

My love to all...

~Lieutenant Lord Cedric Kellinggrave,
in a hastily written note to his parents,
the Duke and Duchess of Landrith

Four hours later
Dovetonwick Court study

Dressed for supper and arms folded, Constantine leaned against the window jamb. The past few hours had not gone as he'd expected. Furthermore, a summons to the study never boded well—particularly mere minutes before dinner. He felt rather like a lad in a skeleton suit called before his father to explain why tadpoles swam about the solarium's fountain.

How else could a six-year-old observe the wiggly creatures' progression into frogs?

An old half barrel behind the manor and under the grape arbor had become the amphibians' new home. Constantine had spent several exciting weeks studying the frogs until the creatures hopped off to a new home.

Even now, when he heard frogs croaking at Dovetonwick Court, he speculated if they were descendants of the tadpoles he'd raised.

Then, just as he did now, Father tried to hide the amused twitch at the corners of his mouth.

Well, things couldn't be so awful if Father was amused.

"What were you thinking? The gossip would've been uncontainable." At six and fifty, only a few strands of silver interspersed Mother's flaxen hair. Fine lines framed her mouth and eyes, revealing she smiled often. In truth, Mother's sense of humor was rather infamous, as were her practical jokes. "Offering her *your* chamber? La, son."

She clearly found no humor in the current situation, however.

"Surely you are aware people would presume you'd ensconced your mistress in your bedchamber, bold as brass, Constantine."

"I don't keep a mistress, Mother."

Constantine couldn't keep the drollness from his tone.

He'd never had the time, inclination, or patience to deal with a demanding woman. Besides, most females possessed an innate aversion to insects, even pretty moths and butterflies.

Except for Miss Roth. Not once had she grimaced, flinched away, curled her lip or little nub of a nose, or cringed.

And his laboratory was chock-full of cringe-worthy specimens.

Arms still folded, he examined a fingernail, then skewed an eyebrow in mock askance.

"Are you suggesting I should begin the practice?" Glancing up, he caught his mother's startled expression and hastily exchanged a glance with Father. "I quite thought you disapproved of such arrangements."

Though theirs had been an arranged marriage, his parents had fallen in love and eschewed the practice so popular with the *ton* of taking lovers. They'd also instilled those values in their children, though Constantine knew full well that his brothers knew their way around a boudoir.

Indigo eyes alight with jollity, Father made a poor attempt to hide his chuckle beneath a closed fist to his mouth and a contrived cough.

Mother gave him an arch look before dismissing Constantine's comment and returning to the issue that had worked her into a fine fettle. Pacing the floor, she flung him a *How could you?* glance.

Surely his mother knew her youngest son well enough to know he hadn't considered beyond his initial impulse. Why others fussed and obsessed over such trivialities, he'd never understand.

Miss Roth needed a bedchamber.

He offered his.

There was nothing more to it.

"Did you consider Charlotte at all, Constantine?" Mother flicked her black lace, hand-painted fan open and waved it before her face. "How your recklessness could affect her wedding?"

Constantine would vow that Charlotte didn't give two wags of a lamb's tail. She would marry her vicar, and they'd live in blissful matrimony all their days.

Or was it happily ever after?

Mother's elegantly plucked winged eyebrows arched in anticipation, her expectant gaze boring into him.

"I've explained the situation, Mother. Nothing untoward was suggested, nor has it occurred. Berkham can vouch for the truth of that. I haven't seen Miss Roth since Edyth escorted her into the house."

Constantine had intended to send a note round to Miss Roth, inquiring after her health, but he'd been detained by one guest or family member after another all afternoon. Before he knew it, it had been time to dress for dinner.

Precisely why he limited his sojourns to Dovetonwick Court.

How was a man expected to get any work done with people wanting to converse all the time? There was something to be said for silence.

"That may be so, Con." Father scratched above his ear, his gaze brimming with wisdom. Gray peppered his sideburns and shock of honey-brown hair. "But you know as well as I do, devious minds don't need more than a hint of impropriety to stir up a scandalous tempest."

Constantine spread his hands wide. "I meant no harm."

In fact, he'd thought himself quite the gallant. Chivalrous and all that claptrap, sacrificing his comfort for a damsel in distress. In general, he wasn't much for courtly posturing. He couldn't even account for his impetuous offer. The words had tumbled off his tongue like water plunging over a fall.

Who would've thought an extra female guest would throw the entire household into a tizzy? But then, what did he know of such matters? Housekeepers, mothers, sisters, and wives attended to such tedious details.

"*You are an old-fashioned fart, Kell.*" Ronan Brockman's mocking accusation, which had led to the ridiculous wager, echoed in Constantine's mind.

Constantine deliberately veered his attention from Brockman's accusing, humor-filled voice to Harvey's glum tones earlier today.

Harvey had informed him shortly after their arrival that his third-story chamber was no larger than a horse stall and contained a single bed.

Under no circumstances would Constantine sleep with knobby-kneed Harvey, friend or not. Harvey might wear a nightshirt to bed, but Constantine didn't.

The implication didn't bear contemplating.

Wouldn't that give the rumormongers a succulent morsel to bandy about?

He almost permitted the grin tugging at the corners of his mouth to bloom into full humor. But that would mean explaining the irregular and somewhat risqué path his thoughts had paraded down to his parents.

He dismissed the notion of sharing a chamber with Harvey, opting instead to utilize his brother Cedric's bedchamber, as Cedric had yet to arrive from London.

Embly had supplied that helpful snippet of information as any good valet worth his pay would've done.

The war secretary seemed reluctant to have his favorite attaché absent from Whitehall. At least that was the official reason Cedric had given in his letter to their parents, explaining he wouldn't arrive until Friday.

Constantine had long suspected the middle Kellinggrave brother was a spy.

Believing Miss Roth snuggly ensconced in his bedchamber, slumbering away the adverse effects of their journey, Constantine had changed into his evening attire in Cedric's room.

"At least Edyth had the good sense to put Miss Roth in her chamber to rest and not yours," Mother said with a particularly vigorous flap of her fan.

Constantine jerked his head up. "She did?"

Why hadn't Embly disclosed that critical detail?

Mother went on as if she hadn't heard him.

"Though I nearly suffered apoplexy when Berkham told me you'd given your chamber to your *female* scrivener." Shaking her elegantly coiffed head, her diamond earrings swinging back and forth in her exuberance, Mother pointed at Constantine. "I'll have the why of *that* from you too, but not presently."

"Quite unusual, my boy," Father put in conversationally. "A female scribe. Is she any good at the craft?"

"Excellent, as a matter of fact." Certainly, that was not pride ringing in his voice.

His mother gave Constantine a sharp look.

Resplendent in ivory and violet silk, the duchess reminded him of an iris in full bloom.

"I cannot leave her in Edyth's chamber unless we pretend Miss Roth is a relative." She put her ebony gloved finger to her chin.

"A distant cousin, perhaps?" She gave a slow nod. "Yes, that might work."

"My dear, you worry too much about what others think." Father gave her a tender smile and put an arm around her shoulders. "My brother will know she's not a cousin on our side."

Yes, Uncle Hayward knew the Kellinggrave family tree

forward and back, up and down, and sideways. Constantine always suspected his father's twin brother's obsession with the family lineage was a façade to cover his desire to find a means to claim the duchy for his wayward, rapscallion son, Martin.

"You could claim Miss Roth is your distant cousin, I suppose, my dear." Father patted Mother's hand.

Shaking his head, Constantine straightened to his full height. "I plan on working while I'm here. If you claim Miss Roth is a cousin, she won't be able to perform her duties."

"Hmph. You should've thought of that. At the very least, you could've informed me you'd hired a female scrivener." Lips pursed, Mother stared across the room in the manner she did when she was scheming. "Perhaps we can claim she's a companion for Edyth now that Charlotte is moving away."

There was a slight catch in her voice.

Mama and Charlotte were extremely close.

"Miss Roth would still be unavailable for my needs," Constantine persisted while trying to squelch a small surge of irritation.

Father raised a sardonic eyebrow, his mouth twitching the merest bit. Again.

"Not *those* needs, Father."

Mother glanced at the brass and marble ormolu mantel clock and snapped her fan shut. "La, it's time for the supper gong."

She speared Constantine a reproachful glance.

"We are not finished with this conversation, Constantine."

Constantine cupped his nape.

This wasn't going at all as he'd planned. He required Miss Roth's scrivener skills to accomplish what he'd intended this week. Another obstacle to his plans was not acceptable.

"What is Miss Roth to do this evening?" he asked. "I

assure you. She does not have a wardrobe that will convince anyone that she is a cousin."

"She'll have to remain in Edyth's chamber until I have time to think this arrangement through. Though I hate fibbing, we'll claim a headache from her travels to explain Miss Roth's absence from supper."

"A little fib to prevent a scandal is perfectly acceptable, my dear." Father nodded and cast a longing glance toward the study door as he patted his stomach. He'd probably missed his midday meal again.

Constantine had inherited his absent-mindedness from his sire.

"Miss Roth can borrow your sisters' gowns. Nita is an excellent seamstress and can make any alterations required." Mother compressed her mouth again in contemplation. "Slippers might be an issue, but we cannot discuss this further at the moment."

"Why not send her home tomorrow?" Father suggested as he adjusted a cuff. "Not all the house guests have arrived. Miss Roth went directly to Edyth's chamber, and Edyth said they didn't encounter anyone on the way up. I doubt anyone knows Miss Roth is here."

"No!" Constantine shook his head and eased the sharpness of his refusal with an apologetic upward sweep of his mouth. "She suffered terrible malaise on the entire trip here. I could not in good conscience make her endure another three days. It would be cruel."

"Yes, I quite agree," Mother conceded, giving him an odd, penetrating look. "I have suffered an unsettled stomach on long journeys. Poor dear. I'll have mint tea and dry toast sent up."

Constantine strode to his father's desk. "I'll just write Miss Roth a quick note and explain the situation."

She wouldn't be happy about being confined to Edyth's chamber, and Constantine couldn't blame her. He'd wager she would be even less happy about pretending to be a companion or distant cousin.

As he flipped the inkwell top open, a thought struck him. Faith Roth might refuse to go along with the subterfuge. What then?

FOUR

As the past two correspondences have returned to me as having an invalid address, I only write this letter to inform you that I fully intend to notify the authorities. I believe something nefarious is afoot—perhaps even something criminal.

I presume the information regarding the child you brought to us six months ago is little more than a fairytale and is as fabricated as your name.

I intend to fully cooperate with the authorities and pray that any way I may have inadvertently contributed to your deceit is rectified when the truth is revealed.

~Mrs. Hester Shepherd, in a stern letter
to John W. Smith (Not his real name.)

Dovetonwick Court
Lady Edyth Kellinggrave's bedchamber
Half past eight the next morning

Am I a prisoner?

Don't be absurd.

Of course, Faith wasn't. Prisoners didn't stay in luxurious rooms and eat succulent meals. Still, she'd basically been forbidden to leave this bedchamber.

Why?

Standing before the window, she admired the intricate gardens below. Had she been permitted her freedom, she'd have spent the morning exploring the lush blossoms and intricate pathways.

Well, if her employer hadn't required her services.

She stifled a sigh and forbid the scowl trying to form.

Surely someone would explain what was going on soon— why she had been asked not to leave Lady Edyth's bedchamber.

Wouldn't they?

Every instinct Faith possessed had urged her to refuse to accompany Lord Constantine.

And lose her position?

No. Faith had worked too hard and sacrificed too much to attain her dream.

"I'm certain you won't have to remain tucked away here much longer, Miss Roth. I'll try to determine the delay at breakfast this morning."

Bestowing a bright smile, Lady Edyth skipped across the pink, yellow, and green floral Axminster carpet. She gave Faith's hand a reassuring squeeze.

She really was a delight. As sweet and kind as she was pretty and unaffected.

A rare thing amongst the *ton*, particularly for a cosseted youngest daughter of a duke.

"I've enjoyed your company, Faith. I hope you will permit

me to call you Faith, and of course, you must call me Edyth or Edie. Charlotte is so much older than I. You and I are closer in age. I am ever so curious to learn how you became Constantine's scribe. I don't mind sharing a chamber with you in the least."

She produced another radiant smile.

The girl possessed a sunny disposition in addition to her chatty nature.

"I appreciate your benevolence, my lady."

What else could Faith say?

She'd been shown to the girl's private chamber and had remained here ever since. Faith had to admit it had been wise of Lady Edyth to ignore her brother's suggestion that Faith use his bedchamber.

The girl was clever and intelligent. And generous. Faith didn't know another aristocrat who would've welcomed a complete stranger into their private sanctuary. Lady Edyth had done so without hesitation and had been nothing but gracious.

"I'll be back as soon as I can, Faith."

With a little wave, Lady Edyth, wearing a youthful pink and lace confection that would've made Faith look like an iced pastry, departed the chamber.

Faith smoothed her palms down the front of her calico gown. It was the least stark of her clothing, and as she was uncertain what was expected of her, she opted for her prettiest gown.

Her still-packed bags stood like three miniature sentinels beside the door. She could read but didn't really feel like it. Unaccustomed to idleness, she wandered to the window again.

This was really too much.

Lord Constantine, at the very least, could speak with her.

Explain what in the blazing bluebells was going on. In truth, she felt rather like a pariah or a woman of questionable moral standards. A female amanuensis was unusual but assuredly not a shun-worthy profession.

Fifteen minutes later, a soft tap echoed at the door.

Faith opened it, unsurprised to see a different maid than last night carrying a breakfast tray.

"Good morning. I've brought you breakfast," the servant said cheerily as she breezed into the room but took care to shut the door behind her.

"Where shall I lay it out for you, miss?"

"No need." Faith shook her head. "I can do it myself. Just place the tray on the window seat."

At least she could gaze outdoors while she ate.

"Very well." In short order, the bubbly maid had set the tray down and retraced her steps to the door. "I'm Alice. Should you need anything, just pull the bell."

She nodded her head toward the pink tasseled bell pull beside the door.

"Thank you."

After she departed, Faith curled up on the charming window seat and ate heartily. She wasn't the sort who lost their appetite or picked at their meals if she was upset. If she was hungry, she ate.

Popping the last bite of strawberry preserve-smothered scone into her mouth, her gaze landed on the brusque note sitting on the night table from Lord Constantine last night. The curt missive requesting she remain secreted away in his sister's bedchamber had not only raised her ire but her curiosity.

Baffled, she'd read the three lines so many times that she'd committed them to memory.

Miss Roth, unexpected circumstances make it necessary for you to remain in my sister's chamber. As soon as a solution has been devised, you shall be informed. Please do not leave Lady Edyth's bedchamber until then.

    CK

Biting the end of a strawberry, Faith glanced at the gilt bronze and ivory marble bedside clock again. Two minutes had crept by with the speed of a slug in molasses in wintertime.

Enough.

After tossing the remaining strawberry on her plate, Faith set aside the tray and climbed to her feet. She wasn't a prisoner or criminal. Whether due to poor planning or communication, however, she bore the brunt of the situation.

Well, no more.

She'd simply find Lord Constantine and demand an explanation.

Unexpected circumstances, indeed.

Surely in a house this size, there was a corner or nook where a pallet might be laid to accommodate Faith. After all, she was accustomed to sharing a bedchamber and didn't require a down mattress. At the academy, four girls typically shared a single room.

Decision made, Faith checked her appearance in the mirror. A tendril had escaped her simple chignon, and after pinning it, she collected the tray. She was perfectly capable of returning a tray to the kitchens.

If she could find her way to the kitchen in this mammoth house, that was. Lady Edyth had taken so many turns and climbed two flights of stairs as she directed Faith to this wing of the mansion.

Closing her eyes, she pictured the path she'd traversed to get to this room. It was simply a matter of reversing course.

Wasn't it?

No time like the present to test her sense of direction. Faith had always enjoyed a challenge. Prayer couldn't hurt either, even for a trivial matter such as finding the kitchens and then searching out Lord Constantine.

A little help would be much appreciated, Lord.

All went well until Faith descended the first flight of stairs and nothing looked the least familiar. Glancing over her shoulder, she skewed her mouth to the side.

Those *were* the stairs she'd climbed yesterday with Lady Edyth.

Weren't they?

Botheration.

She continued down the corridor in the direction she thought she needed to go, then took a left. Nothing but a row of doors on either side met her inspection. Likely guest chambers.

Clearly, she'd taken a wrong turn.

A door opened somewhere nearby, and she hurried to catch whoever it was and ask for their assistance. Even she couldn't be persuaded that the Duke and Duchess of Landrith would appreciate their son's employee creeping about the house when she had been told—quite specifically, in fact—to remain out of sight.

I'm not creeping, she told herself as she hurried along the passage. *I'm simply disoriented.*

Rounding the corner, she caught sight of a gentleman dressed in the first stare of fashion striding in the opposite direction. He whistled as he strode along, his pace casual and unhurried.

"Excuse me, sir." She hurried forward with the cumbersome tray. "I fear I've become turned around and cannot find my way."

He slowly pivoted and, after taking her measure for a trifle too long to be entirely polite, flashed her a rakish grin. "Easy to do in this monstrosity."

Perhaps in his late thirties, he wasn't particularly handsome but possessed interesting features and cool gray eyes. Assessing eyes. Shrewd eyes. There was something familiar about his features too.

Faith would vow he didn't miss anything, and she unexpectedly regretted the impulse to seek his help.

He bent an arm over his abdomen and bowed while giving her a disarming smile.

A tremor of disquiet skittered up her spine.

He might not be as handsome as Lord Constantine, but this man was a practiced rake.

"Martin Kellinggrave, at your service."

Martin Kellinggrave?

One of the dreaded cousins.

Unexpected and unwelcome, genuine disquiet caused Faith to search the corridor behind him.

He hadn't said or done anything untoward, yet Faith wished someone else would come along. In a house supposedly filled to overflowing, servants and guests were unaccountably absent.

Mr. Kellinggrave gave the tray an exaggerated stare. He obviously couldn't figure out why she carried the tray when she wasn't dressed like a maid.

Faith wasn't going to answer his silent question.

"And you are?" he probed, his gaze sliding to the silver cross—a parting gift from Mrs. Shepherd—pinned at her collar before dipping lower.

A shudder reverberated through her.

"I saw you arrive with Constantine yesterday."

Perhaps *he* was the peeper.

His tone grew suggestive. "Are you his *amour*?"

"Certainly not." Of all the gall.

Who was this blackguard?

"*She* is none of your concern, Martin."

Faith barely refrained from yelping in surprise upon hearing Lord Constantine's familiar voice. Her heart soared with relief—what else could the fluttering sensation be?

She half-turned as he approached.

"Constantine." Martin Kellinggrave gave a stiff nod, and his thin smile didn't light his cold eyes. His focus shifted to Faith, and the outer edges of his eyes flared the merest bit. "Since you are unwilling to introduce us, I shall be on my way."

Faith waited until he'd disappeared from sight to face Lord Constantine. "Thank you..."

Her voice trailed off.

Thunder flashed in his eyes, and disapproval was stamped upon his features as he stood, arms akimbo and mouth grim, before her.

He was angry.

At her.

She lifted a shoulder.

"I lost my way," she said needlessly.

"I asked you to remain in Edyth's bedchamber."

"No, my lord, you ordered me to. I am not here to remain isolated and banned as if I were a leper." The tray had become quite heavy, but she'd eat feathers before admitting it to him. "Need I remind you? It was *your* idea for me to accompany you to Dovetonwick Court."

Face taut, he took the tray from her and placed it on a hall table.

"I was taking that below."

"A servant will do so. You're not a domestic in this household and needn't act as if you are."

His tone was guttural, harsh, and his words clipped.

It took a full five heartbeats for Faith to summon a response that wasn't churlish.

"I am accustomed to seeing to my own needs, my lord, and I shan't impose work on someone else that I am perfectly capable of performing myself."

The arrogant, entitled, elitist...prig.

He sighed and scraped his long, ink-stained fingers through his hair.

"I apologize, Miss Roth. It is not you that I am frustrated with but rather the awkward situation that has arisen."

Feeling somewhat mollified, she angled her head. "The dilemma cannot be all that difficult. Does your family object to a female scrivener? Their disapproval is not unexpected, I suppose."

Snorting, he shook his head, then released a grating, empty chuckle. "That is the least of our worries."

"How so?"

"Someone—presumably a guest—overheard me offer you my bedchamber."

The woman wearing blue.

The snoopy busybody. How dare she smudge Faith's reputation when she hadn't met her?

"That person has been busy spreading that savory morsel amongst the guests. At this juncture, we can safely presume..." Lord Constantine pulled a face and brushed three fingers over his forehead.

"Presume what?"

Did she really want to know?

What alternative was there?

When he remained silent, strain accenting the chiseled contours of his face, she sighed.

"I'm not a wilting flower, my lord. I assure you, I shall not weep or swoon."

Regardless, Faith's stomach tightened in anticipation.

"*Swoon*? I should say not." Genuine offense crinkled his forehead that Faith would suggest such a thing.

"*You*, my dear Miss Roth, are the most singular female I know and least likely to indulge in feminine machinations with a fit of the vapors."

Was that a compliment or an insult?

It was so very difficult to tell with this odd man.

In truth, half the time, Faith wasn't certain he knew himself.

"My lord?" Folding her arms, she arched an eyebrow.

A wonder no one had come upon them conversing in what might be misconstrued as an intimate manner. Breakfast might be credited for that welcome reprieve.

No doubt, most of the guests were either still dining or abed.

In general, the upper ten thousand seldom left their comfortable mattresses at an early hour. They didn't know what they had missed. Morning was the most glorious time of day. A gift from the Lord, bringing new hope and opportunities.

"The tale isn't going to tell itself, your lordship."

In for a penny, in for a pound.

Might as well have the whole of it and know what she was up against.

"Yes, well." Lord Constantine cleared his throat while taking a furtive sweep of the corridor. He tucked his chin to his chest, cupped the back of his neck, and glanced up at her through hooded eyes, his expression inscrutable.

Was that chagrin shining there?

Was the confident, arrogant, self-righteous Lord Constantine Kellinggrave embarrassed?

This morsel must be extraordinarily tantalizing, indeed.

"We can presume that most guests have been led to believe, like my cousin just did, that you are my…erm…mistress."

FIVE

*We're hosting an intimate soirée. The details are below.
I do so hope you will be able to come. I've invited our closest
friends. It will be a long overdue reunion. Even Trinity
and Mrs. Shepherd plan to be there.*

~Mrs. Joy Morrisette, in a letter to Faith Roth

Still in the passageway

Of the reactions Faith might've had to the unpleasant confession, Constantine had not expected her to burst into uncontrolled laughter. Not a dainty feminine titter either. No, bent over in glee, she held her ribs and tears of hilarity trickled down her cheeks. She sucked in great gulps of air between irrepressible chortles.

"*Me?*" she gasped, incredulous, her voice pitched to the twelve-foot decorative plasterwork ceiling.

53

Hysterical laughter interrupted her, and several more seconds passed as she struggled to contain her hilarity.

"*Your* mistress? That's utterly, completely, categorically preposterous."

Something that might've been disappointment if Constantine permitted himself to examine the emotion tunneled around his middle. If he had any remaining doubts about whether Faith regarded him with anything other than thinly concealed disdain and dislike, she'd succinctly dispelled that notion.

Nevertheless, no one appreciated being dismissed as inadequate.

He'd never seen her unfettered laughter before, and despite the graveness of the moment, a grin strained to curve his mouth upward. At once, he checked the impulse because, by thunder, despite his scrivener's current jovial state, this was not a laughing matter.

Shaking her head, Faith removed her spectacles and swiped at the moisture pooled in her eyes.

"Someone is making a May game of you, my lord."

Wide doe eyes fringed with thick, sooty lashes and twinkling with merriment gazed into his. She had lovely eyes. Quite stunning, in truth. Soft and warm with flecks of amber and a gold ring around her iris.

Why had Constantine never noticed how beautiful they were before?

It must be the spectacles. They detracted from Faith's pretty eyes.

As she slid the eyeglasses back into place, another round of laughter consumed her.

Eyebrow cocked, he waited for her amusement to subside.

At last, Faith reined her humor under control, and a silly

grin bending her mouth, composed herself. "Surely, you're not serious? We don't even like each other."

That last bit stung, and it oughtn't to have done, for it was the truth.

They rubbed along as well as vinegar and salt.

"I wish I were not"—fervently wished, truth be told—"for both our sakes. Regardless, I regret I am wholly serious. Now we must undo the damage post-haste."

At his poor choice of words, he winced inwardly.

She planted her hands on her hips, drawing his attention to her trim waist. She wore the calico again today. The colorful fabric did something almost wondrous to her hair and skin. That glorious hair would draw many of the male guests' appreciation.

A weird stabbing twisted Constantine's heart, which might've been jealousy if he wasn't wholly immune to the troublesome emotion. He forced his attention elsewhere.

"Please correct me if I misunderstood, my lord, but it sounded as if you just said we must undo the damage? What damage? Until this moment, we haven't spoken to one another since I arrived. And I hardly think your kept mistress would sleep in your sister's bedroom."

Exactly.

No telltale maidenly blush bloomed on her cheeks at the taboo subject's mention.

Faith—when had Constantine begun to think of her thus? —shoved a stray lock of strawberry blonde hair off her porcelain cheek.

"I suggest we ignore the tattle, my lord. It will die down soon enough. I shall need a different place to sleep, of course. Given the difference in our stations, I cannot remain in your sister's bedchamber. I'm not particular, however. A pallet on the floor would suffice."

No, by Juniper, it would not.

How could Constantine stretch out upon his plump mattress when she lay upon a hard floor?

What manner of monster did she think him?

Besides, Mother had contrived what she believed was a foolproof scheme.

It meant deceptiveness—a small, unpleasant cost for the good of all. Or so Constantine tried to convince himself.

What choice had they?

Constantine scratched his temple and tossed another glance up and down the corridor. They really ought to have this conversation someplace that assured privacy rather than here where anyone could come upon them or listen behind a door.

He stepped nearer to Faith and lowered his voice. If anyone overheard them, the game was up, and his siblings and he would be up to their neck in suds.

"My mother has come up with a solution that we believe should stop the unsavory gossip and protect your reputation."

"And your family's as well?" A thread of cynicism leached into Faith's tone.

"Naturally."

No sense in denying the obvious, or rather the real motivation behind Mother's scheme. She was a fair woman—kind and generous—but when it came to her children... Well, the truth was that she became a veritable lioness or mother bear. No one—absolutely *no one*—was spared her wrath when she protected her children.

"Pray tell me, what is this plan, my lord?"

A single line pulled Faith's fine eyebrows together. The smattering of freckles on her cheeks and nose stood out in stark relief, revealing she'd begun to comprehend the tenuousness of the situation.

"It's been decided that you're a distant cousin on my mother's side who's come for Charlotte's wedding. Afterward, you may decide to stay at Dovetonwick Court and become Edyth's companion."

"How very magnanimous," Faith muttered, her tone dry and caustic as ash.

Constantine chose to disregard her acerbity.

"You'll stay in Edyth's room for now, and after the wedding, move to Charlotte's bedchamber until the last guest has departed next week."

He pinched the bridge of his nose, where a headache had begun to throb.

"It will delay our return to London, but it cannot be helped. If anyone should inquire after you, Mother will say you missed your family most dreadfully and returned home."

Nice and neat and convenient.

For the Kellinggraves.

Not so much for Faith, he was honest enough to admit.

"So I am to be a party to a deception and a lie?" Twin spots of color appeared on her high cheekbones, and offense flashed in her eyes. She thrust her chin out and squared her shoulders.

"I am not a deceitful woman, my lord. I was raised to be virtuous and honest. What you ask of me goes against everything I value."

Constantine closed his eyes.

No one, except him, had considered Faith might refuse.

Admiration for her integrity, even though it might mean her ruination, budded behind his ribs.

"I respect your position, Faith."

And Constantine did.

Few people had the moral scruples to stand firm when it proved detrimental to themselves. It complicated matters—

made the situation bloody untenable—but honestly, he was relieved that he didn't have to go along with the farce.

"There is another factor none of you has considered." Faith matched the subdued tenor of her voice to his.

"And that is?" Constantine was positive he, Father, and Mother had gone over every possible scenario.

"A woman eavesdropped at the entrance after we arrived yesterday and may have heard you introduce me as your amanuensis."

Bollocks.

Constantine jerked his head up. "What woman?"

Faith lifted a shoulder. "I don't know. I saw her blue skirts behind the butler. I think perhaps she realized I'd spied her, and she left."

The footman and butler had heard him as well, but their loyalty to the duke and duchess was unquestionable.

"We need to make our way to my mother's private salon. She'll need to be aware of this detail before she puts her plan into play."

If she hadn't already.

"You mean her falsehood?" Fire sparked in Faith's accusing gaze.

Constantine sighed. "I don't like it any more than you do, but it's not just about us. Charlotte's wedding is in a couple of days. I don't want her special day shadowed by scandal, even if it is fabricated. Edyth hasn't had her Come Out yet. As ludicrous and unfair as it is, something of this nature could taint her launch into Society."

Faith stared at the wall for several heartbeats, then met his gaze.

"Very well. We shall speak to the duchess. I'm not sure what good it will do at this juncture. Lies and deceit always weave a web, and sooner or later, one becomes tangled in them. Straightforwardness and candor have always served me well."

Constantine barely kept his eyebrows from soaring to his hairline.

"Yes." Constantine half-choked, half coughed. "With a goodly measure of diplomacy, naturally."

"Naturally."

Footsteps muffled on the lush carpet, Faith started forward. As she walked, she turned her head from side to side, examining the eclectic assortment of gilded framed paintings adorning the walls above the gleaming cherrywood wainscotting. Everything from portraits, still lifes, and landscapes festooned the corridor.

Constantine caught up to her and touched her elbow.

"Thank you, Faith."

She slid him an inquisitive look before returning her attention to the artwork.

"I'm not an ogre, my lord. I understand the implications and repercussions."

"If we encounter anyone, just nod and smile," he cautioned.

She rolled her eyes ceilingward, and Constantine chuckled.

There was the Faith he knew so well. The Faith that used to irritate the blazes out of him, but now... Now he rather appreciated her lack of artifice.

They managed to make it to Mother's salon and only encountered a pair of maids carrying bed linens, a footman bearing a breakfast tray, and Miss Wright fetching a shawl for her mother.

His forefinger knuckle bent, Constantine rapped on the door.

"It's me, Mother. Miss Roth is with me."

"Come in, dear."

He pressed the latch and stepped aside for Faith to enter first. Without hesitation, she swept forward. For the first time, he acknowledged that he admired her intrepidness and boldness. Meeting a duchess could be intimidating, but Faith faced it with her usual unflinching bravado.

Mother sat in her favorite armchair, a breakfast tray on the rosewood tea table before her and an assortment of correspondence on the matching table to her left. Smiling, she removed her pince-nez and set them aside.

"To what do I owe this pleasure so early in the day?"

Likely, she knew perfectly well his and Faith's presence was on account of the taradiddle the family was supposed to spread about with the ease of butter on toast.

Faith bent into a perfectly executed curtsy as he shut the door behind him.

"Your Grace."

After a perfunctory peck on the scented and powdered cheek his mother presented, Constantine said, "Mother, may I introduce Miss Faith Roth? Miss Roth, Her Grace, Mabel Kellinggrave, the Duchess of Landrith."

Adjusting the embroidered coral Spitalfield's shawl about her shoulders, Mother tipped her mouth into a conciliatory smile.

"Miss Roth, I presume my son has explained the delicate situation to you?"

Faith nodded, pulled back to the conversation from her perusal of the salon decorated in shades of yellow and gold, and filled with French giltwood Aubusson tapestry furnishings.

"He has, Your Grace."

"Ah, nonetheless, I sense a *but*." Mother's most skeptical eyebrow rose as her keen gaze swept to Constantine and then back to Faith.

"We have a complication, Mother. Miss Roth observed a woman eavesdropping on us when we arrived yesterday. She may know Miss Roth is my employee, in which case, we cannot claim she is a distant cousin."

"Brazenly eavesdropping?" Eyes narrowing, Mother tapped her manicured fingertips against her thigh.

"Yes, ma'am. For several minutes."

Hands folded at her waist, Faith arranged her features into a serene mien.

"Either Adelle Breadalbane or Ida Looram, I'll wager," Mother said. "Both are immature nincompoops and despicable gossips who would sooner bear a false tale than tell the truth. They are only here because their sisters are Charlotte's bridesmaids. Other than Miss Breadalbane's substantial fortune from her maternal grandmother, neither has anything to recommend them."

Mother turned her full attention on Faith. To Faith's credit, she didn't lower her eyes or blush.

"When did you notice her spying on you, Miss Roth?"

Faith closed her eyes for a moment. When she opened them, they were clear and focused.

"It was just before Lord Constantine told Lady Edyth I was his amanuensis."

"Hmm." One finger to her chin, Mother focused on the opposite wall.

Constantine knew that expression. She was plotting something again.

Mother never was one to accept defeat. She would've made a splendid general.

"I have it!" Her smile was positively jubilant.

Faith gave a little start and exchanged a disconcerted glance with him.

"Amanuensis. Affianced," she said proudly.

Good God. She wasn't suggesting...?

No! Positively no.

SIX

While cleaning and organizing the office of my predecessor, I came upon a file that had slipped behind a cabinet and contained a letter you sent nearly twenty years ago. You expressed concern regarding the circumstances surrounding a child placed into your care. It appears my predecessor made a few initial inquiries but, for reasons unknown, didn't finish the investigation.

At this late date, I dare say, the trail has run cold. However, if you still have concerns or possess additional information, I am at your service.

I apologize on behalf of my predecessor.

~Detective Cyril Dankworth, in a letter
to Mrs. Hester Shepherd

**Still in the Duchess of Landrith's private salon
Ten strained seconds later**

Impossible. I shan't do it.

Utterly nonplussed, Faith couldn't prevent her slack jaw as she gaped incredulously at the duchess. Her heart cavorting behind her ribcage, she cast a panicked glance toward Lord Constantine.

It gave her a great deal of satisfaction to see his strong jaw unhinged and his flabbergasted expression. He was as flummoxed by his mother's preposterous suggestion as Faith was.

"Affianced?" Faith croaked through the tightness strangling her throat. "Are you suggesting his lordship and I *pretend* to be betrothed?"

Good Lord.

The scheme was as cliché as a penny novel.

"Precisely." Her Grace beamed as if it were the simplest solution, and everyone should be as thrilled as she. She waved her hand in the air, the gemstones on three fingers glinting with the movement. "Given the distance from you and the eavesdropper, and that the Misses Breadalbane and Looram don't have the acumen of a potato between them, I'm positive neither knows what an amanuensis is. Whomever our nefarious spy is, she'll presume she misheard."

"Now, Mother."

Lord Constantine perched on the arm of the settee opposite her in a rather charming and childish fashion, giving Faith a glimpse of the boy he'd once been.

His buff-colored trousers pulled tautly over muscular thighs. For a man obsessed with science and bugs, he was remarkably fit. Hadn't Mr. Camberg-Trainer mentioned his lordship trained at Gentleman Jackson's thrice weekly?

Why, pray tell, was Faith noticing those disquieting facts at this critical juncture?

Lord Constantine gave his mother a cajoling smile—one

that, no doubt, he'd used to finagle his way out of trouble many times before.

"Be reasonable, Mother dearest. It's one thing to ask Miss Roth to play the role of a cousin, but my betrothed?" A deep, resonating chuckle bubbled forth as he shook his head and a lock of sandy blond hair flopped onto his forehead. "I cannot agree to the farce. The scandal will be far worse when no marriage takes place."

"Yes." Faith gave a vigorous nod. "He's right. The ton will descend upon that inconvenient truth like vultures on rotting carrion. Besides, I'm not nobility. I'm an orphan, raised in a foundling home. I have no idea who my parents were."

She was no fool.

The real scandal would be a duke's son's betrothal to a nobody.

Worse than a nobody.

A discarded orphan with no breeding or dowry.

Probably, people would mistakenly assume a love match.

Faith barely controlled a snort of horrified hilarity.

Love match?

Anyone with eyes in their heads would know that farcical twaddle for the colossal lie it was. Neither Faith nor Lord Constantine were good enough actors to fool anyone into believing such balderdash.

More often than not, she and his lordship were at odds.

"Pshaw. Stuff and nonsense." A thread of steel entered Her Grace's tone. "As there's been no formal announcement, we can later claim the arrangement was discreetly terminated. It's only for the duration of the house party, in any event."

Only for the...

This was Faith's life she was so carelessly arranging.

Did this woman always get her way?

Faith squelched her eye roll and the pursing of her lips.

Barely.

Of course, the duchess did.

Didn't most aristocrats? One way or another. By power and influence, or bribery and extortion.

The Duchess of Landrith gazed at Faith as if she expected her to offer profuse thanks for the honor of partaking in a despicable farce.

"Respectfully, Your Grace, I shan't do it."

Faith clenched her hands so tightly that her fingertips grew numb. "I cannot participate in such a deception."

How many times had Mrs. Shepherd drilled into her charges that *the Lord detests lying lips*?

Faith might not be directly lying, but by going along with a falsehood, she was an accomplice and every bit as guilty.

His lordship grazed a hand down his jaw, his green eyes as turbulent as a forest during a windstorm. He was no happier about this debacle than Faith was.

"Miss Roth is correct, Mother. A false betrothal goes too far. I doubt anyone would believe the ruse."

Faith shot him a caustic glance from under her eyelashes. *The boor*.

It was one thing for her to conclude the subterfuge implausible, but for Lord Constantine to vocalize that fact? Well, it chafed.

Still, he'd agreed with Faith and, in doing so, opposed his mother. A warm sensation heated Faith's belly that he'd championed her. For certain, it was a trivial matter, but nonetheless, she'd not been left alone against the powerful woman.

Eyes snapping with reproach, the duchess regally angled her chin.

"Not *too* far to protect my children and this family's reputation." An unyielding I-shan't-take-no-for-an-answer inflection entered her voice. "Please enlighten me on other alternatives that can be hastily implemented?"

"I'm sure we will think of something." Lord Constantine wrinkled his forehead. "Perhaps Miss Roth can stay at the inn in the village?"

It was all Faith could do to not turn an accusing glare upon him. So much for an ally. She wouldn't be here if he hadn't been so stubborn and determined to terminate her employment. She'd be quietly working away on his notes in London.

"So my guests can speculate that you moved your mistress there to give the appearance of respectability, Constantine?"

Flames of humiliation licked at Faith's cheeks.

Hearing herself called a mistress, even if all parties knew it wasn't so, was degrading.

The duchess wasn't one to mince words, was she?

"I can hardly force Miss Roth to participate in the ploy, Mother." Irony dripped from each melodious syllable.

"Of course you can, dear boy." She gave Constantine a smile one might bestow on a simple-minded waif.

"It's quite simple. Miss Roth does as I ask, or you terminate her employment, Constantine."

Faith gasped, her gaze flying to mesh with his lordship's.

He wouldn't agree to his mother's coercion.

Would he?

Did she want to work for a man that would?

The answer came swift and sure.

No. Not even to fulfill a lifelong dream.

Lord Constantine shot to his feet, a vein throbbing in his left temple.

"Now, see here. I appreciate what you are trying to do, Mother, but using extortion demeans you. Miss Roth is my employee, and only I determine her continued status."

Coercion was perfectly acceptable when *he* was the instigator.

A series of three rapid knocks echoed at the door, but before the duchess could bid enter, a distraught Lady Edyth flew into the room. Face flushed and eyes overly bright, she stopped dead in her tracks, a hand pressed to her collarbone when she saw her brother and Faith.

"Oh. I didn't know you were in here." She lowered her hand and fisted her skirt.

"Come, Edyth." Her features softening in concern, the duchess indicated the other chair. This was a woman who truly cared for her children. An oddity amongst *le beau monde*. "Tell me what has you in a dither, my dear."

"I shall excuse myself." Where Faith would go, she had no idea. It didn't seem right to return to Lady Edyth's bedchamber, and she had no desire to mingle with the elite guests. Guests who might very well be talking about her even now.

She headed toward the door, nonetheless.

The wisest thing to do would be to return to London, post haste.

Her stomach wobbled at the idea of another three days of coach travel and staying at inns unaccompanied. Faith would do it though. She wasn't a wilting flower. No, by heavens, she wasn't.

She was Faith Stephanie Hannah Shephard Roth. Orphaned and raised in a foundling home, she had worked hard, studied even harder, and managed to gain a position in a male-dominated field. A trifling coach ride was nothing.

"As shall I." Lord Constantine bowed.

"No. You should stay. It concerns both of you," Lady Edyth said softly.

Faith pivoted back toward her.

Pity shone in Lady Edyth's eyes.

"I am sorry, Miss Roth." She swept her gaze to her brother. "Adelle Breadalbane is telling all and sundry that you've again demonstrated your lack of decorum and refusal to abide by society's strictures, Constantine, by bringing your mistress to your sister's wedding."

"Adelle Breadalbane shall henceforth find herself shunned by all the most prestigious names." Though the Duchess of Landrith's tone was perfectly modulated, each word held an uncompromising promise.

The door flew open again, and a pretty woman with light brown eyes and hair barged in. Her virginal white gown, trimmed in cornflower blue ribbon, complimented her coloring.

This must be Lady Charlotte, and she appeared on the cusp of tears.

Her agitated gaze alit accusingly on her brother, shifted to Faith, then veered back to Lord Constantine.

"Is it true, Con? Did you bring your mistress to my wedding?" A crystalline droplet trickled down her ivory cheek. "How could you, Con? Everyone is talking about it."

"Of course not, Lottie. You offend me by suggesting such a vulgar thing." Lord Constantine strode to his sister and drew her into his arms. "Miss Roth is my scrivener. Nothing more."

He needn't keep hammering that point home.

Lady Charlotte dabbed at her eyes.

"It matters naught. *They*"—she shot a half distraught, half contemptuous glance toward the door—"believe it is true."

"'Tis precisely as I feared," Her Grace said, patting Lady Edyth's hand. "If this isn't nipped in the bud..." The duchess turned that compelling gaze upon Faith. "It would only be for a few days, Miss Roth."

"What would be?" Lady Charlotte asked, confusion pleating her brow.

"A faux betrothal between your brother and Miss Roth."

"Mother." Lord Constantine gave her a steely look hedged with a warning. "We've already discussed this."

"Oh, yes. That would most assuredly do it." Lady Edyth gave an excited bob of her head as Lady Charlotte clasped her brother's hands.

"Please, Con." Biting her lip, Lady Charlotte cut a troubled glance to the closed door again. "You know the ugliness the *ton* is capable of. It would protect Miss Roth too."

His jaw worked as he considered her point.

When he leveled that tumultuous verdant gaze upon her, Faith felt it to her core. He might've reached out and brushed those ink-stained fingertips over her cheek, so unsteady was her cavorting pulse.

"I'll leave it up to you," he silently said across the room.

She heard him as clearly as if he'd shouted it from beside her.

It *was* the best solution.

For everyone.

For her.

Unfair.

Why should Faith compromise her principles because of a bunch of low-minded tattlemongers? Closing her eyes for two tick-tocks of the gilded cherubim mantel clock, she sent a silent prayer to heaven.

Forgive me, Lord, for what I am about to do.

It would take much longer for Faith to forgive herself.

"I'll do it."

She opened her eyelids, unsurprised to find four pairs of eyes staring at her, each brimming with a different emotion.

Her Grace's with supreme satisfaction.

Lady Charlotte with gratitude.

Lady Edyth with relief.

And Constantine's with sorrow and regret.

Because Faith had been forced into this untenable situation or because he'd have to pretend to be the doting affianced?

Regardless, Faith forced her stiff lips into a semblance of a smile, though she rather suspected she resembled a gargoyle and not a blissfully engaged young woman.

"I'll pretend to be Lord Constantine's betrothed, but only for the house party's duration."

SEVEN

As I've explained before, without proof of Bernadette Rennison's death, the inheritance her grandfather left in trust for her is inaccessible. Let me be perfectly clear: that includes access by relatives—blood or otherwise—wishing to initiate inheritance claims.

The terms of the trust do not provide a limitation for this protective provision. However, should there be a presumption of death, and, henceforth, a legal declaration of death for Miss Rennison—signed by the appropriate authorities—a successor beneficiary has been named.

I am certain you understand I cannot divulge the identity of said beneficiary, nor any further details regarding the trust. Nor shall I answer further correspondences from you. At this juncture, communications present a conflict of interest.

If you have information regarding Miss Rennison's disappearance that leads you to believe she is deceased, I advise you to contact the authorities immediately.

~Mr. Barnaby Clipplechap, Solicitor, in

a fourth terse letter to Mr. Aloysius Petheringham

Dovetonwick Court drawing room
Early evening

For the fourth time in ten minutes, Constantine speared a covert glance toward the drawing room's entrance. The guests had gathered for a glass of wine or ratafia before supper, and Edyth and Faith had yet to make an appearance.

After Faith's magnanimous concession this morning, his mother and sisters had whisked her away to make her *presentable*. The despair in her big brown eyes, magnified by her spectacles' lenses, was a mule kick to his gut.

His strong-willed, independent employee had sacrificed her principles to help people she didn't know.

Faith Roth possessed innate decency and integrity Constantine had rarely seen. As much as he grudgingly admired her abilities as a scrivener and even her ability to match wits with him—no easy task—the awareness of her depth of character unlocked something unidentifiable deep within him.

In truth, something he did not desire to examine as closely as his specimens under a microscope. He mightn't like what he found or be prepared to deal with the conclusions.

Lifting his glass to his mouth, he scanned the guests over the rim. Several elegantly attired *le beau monde* members peered in his direction but swiftly averted their gazes when caught staring.

He took a sip of superb wine, welcoming the liquid sliding down his taut throat.

His throat and neck muscles ached from the restraint he'd

displayed today. Not once had he told anyone to bugger themselves and had, in fact, managed an insincere smile several times.

Now that was an accomplishment he could be proud of.

"You look a bit worse for the wear, old chap," Harvey murmured beneath his breath for Constantine's ears alone as he sidled up.

Constantine flung him a swift, hard sideways glance. "It's been a troublesome day."

"So I've heard." A devilish twinkle in his eyes, Harvey gave a lopsided grin. "The house is a veritable bee hive with rumors and speculations buzzing about. I've heard no less than four very intriguing scenarios. However, being the considerate friend that I am, I'll spare your sensibilities and shan't share the details."

"How magnanimous of you," Constantine replied drolly.

A chum from university, Harvey was a good friend and a social equal, but he never missed a chance to have a little fun at Constantine's expense. Particularly when it came to romance. Or rather, Constantine's *lack* of romantic interludes.

Evidently, now that Harvey was madly in love—he felt it his duty to assist Constantine along that same tumultuous pathway.

No, thank you very much.

Constantine had seen what love did to levelheaded, sensible men.

It was embarrassing.

No man should be that vulnerable or malleable.

"That tick in your jaw is a dead giveaway that you're piqued." Harvey waggled his eyebrows before taking a not-so-delicate sip from his glass.

"As I said, it's been an irksome few hours." He cut his

friend a sardonic glance. "And a particularly exasperating past couple of minutes."

Constantine raked the room with a censorious gaze. His generalized disapproval was unfair. Not everyone present was an obnoxious chinwag. After all, these were his parents' closest friends and family, and many were decent, considerate people.

Yes, but all it takes is one proverbial bad apple to spoil the bunch.

"So what *is* the plan, my friend?" Harvey asked a trifle too innocently. Likely as not, he knew exactly what had transpired and the ruse about to commence.

After another stolen glance at the doorway, Constantine quirked an eyebrow. "*Plan*? I cannot think what you mean."

"Hmph. Not going to give it away, eh?" Harvey eyed Constantine up and down, and another grin threatened to divide his face. "By Jove, you are turned out pretty...a veritable first tulip of fashion. I believe this is the first time I've seen you wear that shade of green."

He motioned to Constantine's borrowed Pomona green and gold waistcoat.

Constantine glanced downward.

More of Mother's infernal strategy.

How did she concoct this drivel?

His and Faith's attire would *match* tonight, a silent testament to their upcoming *union*.

Bollocks to that.

Mark his words; this would not end well. Perhaps it saved a bit of chaos at present, but deception had consequences.

Constantine wanted to confide in his friend, but he'd promised not to reveal anything until this evening when he *accidentally* let it slip that he and Faith were betrothed within earshot of the tattlemongers.

Namely, Miss Adelle Breadalbane, who hereafter would be

struck from every polite society invitation list. The loose-lipped girl was about to learn the consequences of spreading tattle about powerful peers.

The other gossips present would do the rest.

By the time everyone regathered in the drawing room after dinner, the faux betrothal would be on every tongue. Lord Constantine Kellinggrave and Miss Faith Roth would be officially engaged for the next few days.

He scratched the side of his jaw.

What would this charade do to their working relationship?

Would Faith continue in his employ after the fiasco was over?

He wanted her to.

It struck him then like a lightning bolt to his chest. In truth, he couldn't fathom what his days would be like without her there. He'd even come to appreciate their ever-so-polite bickering. Mayhap he'd gone soft in the head.

"Careful, old man, you have that glint in your eye that Ronan Brockman had before he toppled bum over boots into love. The same gleam you vowed you saw in my eyes, not more than a week ago." Harvey pointed to his almost black eyes, alive with satisfied amusement.

"Don't be an arse, Harvey."

"Tit for tat." Harvey laughed in what might've been a slightly diabolical fashion. "I confess, this will be most enjoyable to watch play out." After slapping Constantine on the shoulder, he wandered away.

"My dear, try not to be so obvious." Mother had edged to his side, her hand loosely clasping Father's arm. "I vow you've looked at the doorway a dozen times so far."

Wouldn't that give credence to his role as a devoted, lovesick swain?

He swigged the last of his wine.

God save him from such twaddle.

"Just stick to the plan, Constantine, and everything should trot along quite nicely." Mother angled her head toward Lord and Lady Coventry, close friends of hers and the duke's.

"I hope you are right, my pet." Father gave her hand an affectionate pat.

He wasn't the only one.

No doubt, the grand entrance was about to commence.

Before Constantine had finished the thought, Edyth and Faith fairly floated into the room, arm in arm. They made a lovely contrast: Edyth, fair-haired and wearing white, silver, and pink, and Faith's brilliant reddish-blonde hair complemented by her seafoam-green, gold, and peach gown. A coral and pearl necklace graced her swan-like throat, and matching earrings dangled from her delicate ears.

A pointed elbow jabbing his ribs restarted Constantine's stalled breathing.

"Close your mouth, dear. You're gaping like a beached bass," Mother whispered out the side of her mouth while maintaining a benevolent expression, welcoming smile, and a nonchalant rhythmic swish of her brisé fan.

Father's amused chuckle confirmed he'd also seen Constantine's lapse into imbecility.

So glad he provided a source of amusement for his family.

For a man accustomed to being in control and engaging in logic, this sojourn into emotional chaos was most unpleasant.

The focus of every eye in the room, Faith appeared a trifle overwhelmed.

Her silky hair had been swept off her neck and twisted into an intricate knot with a few curls left at her temples. For the first time since Constantine had known her, she did not wear her spectacles, and the vision she presented caused a ball of possessiveness to coil in his gut.

"Go on." Mother nudged him again.

Subtle as a rhinoceros at tea.

He needed no further urging to claim Faith as his and to execute the *plan*. Striding forward, a sincere smile of pleasure arced his mouth. He bowed before his sister and Faith.

"Edyth. You are a vision." Constantine shifted his attention to Faith. "As are you, Faith."

Nearby, someone gasped at his usage of her given name.

Good.

Step one completed.

He'd presumed familiarity that went beyond acceptable boundaries except for specific relationships. For instance, a betrothed couple.

Playing the role of a captivated beau, he turned and presented Edyth and Faith each with an elbow. "Allow me to escort you."

Exchanging a wide-eyed glance—he swore Faith was on the verge of bursting into laughter—the women slipped their gloved hands into the crook of his elbows.

Amid stares and whispers, they made their way to the Duke and Duchess of Landrith.

Conversations faded as the guests focused on the trio.

Charlotte and her soon-to-be husband, Wilfred Howerton, had joined Mother and Father.

His older sister fairly glowed with happiness, as did Howerton.

Only Cedric and Leopold, the ducal heir, were missing from the happy familial tableau. Both were expected to arrive tomorrow. Constantine hid a grimace when he considered their reactions to his false engagement.

They'd fall over themselves with hilarity.

He would worry about that later. For now, he must conform to the plan. Pretending that this was the first time Faith met both of his parents, Constantine swiftly performed introductions.

Having been apprised of the situation, Father bent over Faith's hand and winked. He had always been one who enjoyed a good hoodwinking.

"It is an absolute pleasure to finally meet you, Miss Roth. Constantine has told us so many delightful things about you." He slid his son a mischief-filled glance. "I don't believe I've ever seen him so smitten."

Constantine had never been smitten. Or bewitched. Or besotted.

Emotional rubbish.

Father's ploy worked, however.

A buzz of excitement began near them and quickly spread to the entire room as people speculated about what the duke meant.

Adelle Breadalbane inched closer and closer until her sister, Amelia, stopped her with a stern glance and something hastily whispered in her ear, which caused Adelle to glower and thrust out her lower lip as if she were a petulant six-year-old.

"I am so glad you could make it for our wedding," Charlotte said, bathing Wilfred with a look of adoration.

Wilfred kissed her forehead in such a tender gesture Constantine wanted to tug at his neckcloth. Public shows of affection were not *de rigueur*.

"Ahem." One elegant eyebrow arched, Mother gave Constantine a pointed look.

Ah, yes. The crucial moment had arrived.

Gazing deep into Faith's eyes—those big, chocolatey brown eyes fringed with sooty lashes, so warm and mesmerizing a man could drown in them— he raised her hand to his mouth.

Her peach-tinted lips parted in a perfect display of maidenly surprise and anticipation.

She was quite an accomplished actress.

He'd never have guessed she possessed such talent.

Holding her hand an inch from his lips, he murmured, "Soon, we'll be planning our wedding, my love."

EIGHT

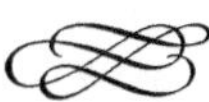

Our family has recently received information that leads us to believe a nefarious relative absconded with our dear sister many years ago and placed her in the foundling home and school you oversee. We are hopeful that Bernadette is alive and well and that we can be reunited.

This relative was named John Smith and would have told you that she was orphaned, and her relatives did not want to be responsible for her care as she'd been born out of wedlock. The latter is untrue.

Do you know where Bernadette is, what name she goes by now, and how we may contact her? We so want to find her.

~Mr. Aloysius Petheringham,
in a letter to Mrs. Hester Shepherd

Dovetonwick Court dining room
Thirty minutes later

Smoothing her monogrammed serviette over her lap while commanding her frolicking stomach to settle, Faith surreptitiously examined either side of the long, elaborate formal dining table. She had no fewer than four forks and three knives, but thanks to Mrs. Shepherd's thorough deportment education, Faith knew what each was used for.

Accustomed to such lavish displays, the other guests laughed and chatted as they settled into their assigned seats or took a sip of wine.

In truth, a glass of wine might help take the edge off Faith's nerves, but she didn't tolerate spirits. Within minutes of partaking, she acquired a stuffy nose and became flushed and nauseous.

An ostrich egg in a canary nest would be less out of place than she felt at the moment.

A stately woman halfway down the table smiled in her direction. The groom's widowed aunt, Mrs. Eustasia Peagilly, if Faith recalled correctly from their introduction several minutes before. Mrs. Peagilly had lived a colorful and exotic life, traveling the world with her three husbands.

Despite the pretense of acceptance by the Landriths' guests and family, Faith wasn't a naive debutante and didn't fool herself. She'd seen the astonished expressions, the swift whispers behind hands and fans, and even now, the calculating or speculative glances aimed toward her and Constantine, who was seated to her right.

She could practically hear them.

Who is she?

Is she an aristocrat?

I've never seen her before.

Who are her connections?

You don't think Lord Constantine is marrying a...nobody? A commoner?

At the duchess's insistence, Faith must address Constantine by his given name to lend credence to their *little* charade.

Little?

Perhaps trivial or inconsequential to the Kellinggraves.

But for Faith, this was a life-altering situation. In truth, she feared the consequences would not be for the better. How could it be for a woman of her station?

For a few heartbeats, nerves overcame her, and she fisted the fine linen serviette. Drawing a steadying breath, she willed her equanimity to return as she deliberately relaxed each finger grasping the cloth in turn. She, Faith Stephanie Hannah Shephard Roth, had made a commitment and would see her part through.

Faith might be a lowborn orphan, but she was a woman of integrity and honor.

The duchess had put aside custom and seated Constantine beside Faith. Likely, advancing the ruse and not a kind demonstration of benevolence had motivated the duchess.

Regardless, having him near bolstered Faith's confidence. Peculiar how a man that had her at sixes and sevens most days had become a source of security.

Seemingly of its own volition, her focus shifted to the Duchess of Landrith, only to find the imperious lady regarding her with a contemplative, but not calculating, expression. Her Grace tilted her chin the merest fraction—in approval?—before signaling for the soup to be served.

A subtle aroma of sandalwood, cedar, and cloves wafted to Faith, and she lowered her chin as a secret, nascent smile pulled her mouth upward at the corners.

For the first time that she was aware, Constantine wore cologne.

Very pleasant cologne too.

At Lady Charlotte's insistence—she really was a dear—Faith, too, wore a splendid fragrance at her wrists and behind her ears. Given the perfume's crystal cobalt bottle, she had no doubt that the scent's cost was quite dear.

Faith almost—*almost*—dared to believe she was as refined and elegant as her borrowed clothes and jewelry portrayed her.

She knew the truth, however.

As the old adage went, you cannot turn a sow's ear into a silk purse.

It took more than an elegant coiffure, expensive perfume, pretty jewels, and a confection of a gown to transform one into a lady.

On the other hand, Constantine had made a brilliant transformation from an engrossed, slightly eccentric scientist to a regal lord. She fully expected he'd be recognized by the Royal Society of London for Improving Natural Knowledge at some juncture. He really was quite brilliant, but she'd taken care not to tell him that.

He was already impossible.

If he believed she admired him—purely professionally, of course—he'd be intolerable.

As if sensing he consumed Faith's thoughts, Constantine leaned near and spoke into her ear. His warm breath caused a shiver to scuttle across her shoulders.

"You're doing magnificently, Faith."

Yes, because refraining from running screaming from a room was praiseworthy.

He squeezed her hand beneath the table's cover, and she met his eyes. She found none of the typical impatience and mockery she'd become accustomed to.

What was he about?

No need to overplay the devoted swain. No one would

believe the scientific-minded, I'd-rather-be-researching Lord Constantine Kellinggrave was suddenly waxing poetic.

Still, he had called her *my love* in the drawing room.

And he'd managed to sound quite authentic.

Edyth had grinned like a cat in the cream, and two other young ladies looked as if they'd eaten spoiled fish. Even the Duke and Duchess of Landrith had shared a speaking look. The kind that people who knew each other well and no words were necessary used.

In point of fact, the entire exchange had been disconcerting.

Tonight, a gleam shone in the enigmatic green depths of Constantine's eyes that Faith could not discern. Her heart gave the queerest flutter in response, and the smile curving her mouth might've been a genuine reaction to the magnetism between them.

Unanticipated and perilous.

This was an act. Nothing more.

Faith would be a fool to consider it anything else.

To those assembled, his whispering in her ear would be regarded as a tender exchange and no doubt strengthen the perception of a couple in love.

Which was the plan. Of course, it was. Every look, every touch, every word was calculated to advance the agenda precisely outlined by the Duchess of Landrith.

Then why did something akin to disappointment settle upon Faith's shoulders, shrouding her in discontentment? She, who had always wanted a career? Had determined to never be dependent upon a man who, on the slightest whim, might cast her aside.

Was that what happened to her mother?

Mrs. Shepherd confessed to knowing very little about Faith's parentage.

A man brought her to the academy when she was scarcely more than a toddler, claiming she was an unwanted, illegitimate orphan. As Mrs. Shepherd had with all her wards, she'd given Faith a new name and identity to help ensure Faith's future.

"I expect the initial shock of our betrothal will dissipate in a day or two," he said, his face so near that she noticed the gold flecks in his eyes and the fine lines framing the corners for the first time. "Assuredly, Charlotte's wedding will once again take center stage, and we'll be forgotten."

As unlikely as Faith discovering who her family was or why she'd been abandoned.

"Where are your spectacles?" Constantine asked beneath his breath. "Are you able to see without them?"

"In my chamber, and yes, I can manage well enough."

More than well enough, truth be told.

Constantine bestowed a disarming, almost roguish, smile upon her and, with another gentle squeeze to her fingers, turned to answer the question boisterous Lady Baumgartner had put to him.

Faith stared at his aristocratic profile for a heartbeat.

Since when did Lord Constantine Kellinggrave practice flirtation?

"What an unexpected surprise, Miss Roth. Neither you nor Cousin Constantine hinted that you were affianced when I came upon you in the corridor."

Botheration.

She recognized that condescending voice.

Because we weren't.

Faith directed her attention to the gentleman on her left.

Martin Kellinggrave.

Would that the duchess had seated him elsewhere. The

stable, for instance. Faith's nerves were already on edge. Dining with this boor beside her all night would stretch her etiquette to the farthest extreme.

He regarded her coolly, inquisitiveness in his unremarkable brown eyes. He clearly believed she owed him an explanation.

She hadn't liked him the first time they met, and the penetrating way he stared at her now made her all the warier of the man, Kellinggrave cousin or not.

"We didn't want to detract from Lady Charlotte's big moment," she said, leaving it at that.

Another clever fabrication of the duchess's to explain the secrecy surrounding Faith and Constantine's unofficial betrothal.

Hoping he'd take the obvious clue that she would rather eat the white soup than converse, she picked up her spoon. She wouldn't rather eat. Her stomach hadn't stopped cartwheeling since she walked into the drawing room and saw Constantine.

Unaccustomed to seeing him togged out in evening finery, she hadn't recognized him for an instant. She'd gazed past him, only to have her attention jerked back to the handsome man staring at her with an expression between flabbergasted and puzzled.

Apparently, he'd been as surprised at her transformation as she was at his.

Constantine had quite literally taken her breath away. His valet had even managed to tame his unruly blond locks, and he presented the epitome of masculine beauty.

Why hadn't she noticed his handsomeness before?

Well, she usually had her spectacles on when near him, and they distorted her vision. She didn't need her eyesight corrected but believed the lenses made her appear older and more professional. Little did her employer know Faith slipped them on as she entered the house for work each morning, and she'd become quite good at looking above the lenses while she worked.

"A marriage and a betrothal for this branch of the Kellinggraves. The duke and duchess must be utterly delighted." The look Martin Kellinggrave leveled their graces, first the duke and then the duchess, wasn't altogether congratulatory.

"I'm sure." What else was Faith to say? "How are you related to Constantine?"

Better to change the subject.

Taking a spoonful of flavorful soup, she glanced toward the head of the table.

Eyes slightly narrowed, the Duke of Landrith regarded Martin Kellinggrave, his expression grave.

Hmm, something more than met the eye went on here.

"Constantine didn't tell you? How remiss of him, as we are soon to be family." Martin Kellinggrave arranged his features into exaggerated puzzlement. "We are cousins. Our fathers are twins. My sisters and father arrive tomorrow."

Spoon at her mouth, Faith paused. "Twins? I wasn't aware."

There was much about her faux betrothed's family she did not know.

"Indeed," Martin Kellinggrave said with a peculiar inflection in his tenor. He lifted his spoon. "My father was born a mere two minutes after Uncle Harland." A cynical smile skewed his mouth. "In Seneca's words, 'Fate rules the affairs of mankind with no recognizable order.'"

Did envy make his words a trifle starchy?

As fifth in line, he was as likely to inherit the duchy as she was to come into a fortune.

Nonexistent.

"Personally, Mr. Kellinggrave, I don't believe in fate. I'd rather put my faith in God."

Faith returned Mrs. Peagilly's friendly smile.

There was an ally. Faith felt certain of it.

Did *she* know the whole truth?

Charlotte or Willard might've confided in her, but the more people who knew about the farcical betrothal, the greater chance of exposure.

"Interesting." Sitting back, Martin Kellinggrave scrutinized Faith until she nearly squirmed in her seat.

The man really was insolent.

Did she have a speck of soup on her lip?

"So, my scientific cousin is marrying a religious zealot?" Martin slanted Constantine a considering, almost suspicious look. "I wouldn't have thought the two were compatible."

"Zealot?" A smile of sincere amusement curved Faith's mouth. "No."

"No?" he fairly mocked, and to Faith's horror, she longed to slap the smirk off his face.

Instead, she tortured the poor serviette again. The laundress would never get the wrinkles out.

She owed Martin no explanation. Still... "Science and faith are not mutually exclusive."

A footman removed her bowl, and she seized the opportunity to turn her attention to Constantine.

Martin Kellinggrave was not someone she wanted to further her acquaintance with.

Constantine gave his cousin a cursory glance before flashing her a blinding smile.

"Walk with me in the gardens this evening, *darling*." Humor darkened his eyes to the color of a forest at twilight. "With the Chinese lanterns lit, it's quite romantic."

He was taking this courting business to heart, wasn't he?

Well, two could play this game.

She laid her hand atop his, where he had rested it upon the table.

"How can I refuse such a tempting invitation, sweetheart?"

NINE

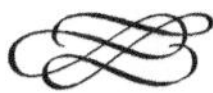

I write with disconcerting information that I haven't shared previously. I take great care to preserve the identities of those who entrust girls to my care. However, given the circumstances and my growing unease, I must divulge confidential facts.

A man named John Smith brought you to Haven House. After a few months, he ceased paying the fees for your care and essentially disappeared. I was unable to ever contact him again. From the outset, I had a niggling suspicion that something wasn't as it ought to be and contacted a detective in London about my concerns, even paying him a retainer. After our initial exchange, I never heard from him and presumed he found no evidence of foul play.

However, I recently received correspondence from Detective Cyril Dankworth saying he found a file about your case that had been misplaced twenty years ago. That same week, a letter arrived from a Mr. Aloysius Petheringham, claiming to be a relative of yours.

I do not believe the timing is coincidental.

We must speak at length and soon. I feel it is rather

urgent. In the meanwhile, do not trust anyone—not even Mr. Petheringham.

~Mrs. Hester Shepherd, in an
urgent missive to Miss Faith Roth

Dovetonwick Court drawing room
After dinner

Constantine intended to take the air as much for his sake as Faith's. A lengthy walk was in order too, all the while staying visible from the house to prevent tattle. Someone took to the rosewood pianoforte, and a handful of guests meandered near to listen or sing along.

With Faith on his arm, he drew abreast of his mother, dazzling this evening in a teal and gold gown as she presided over her domain.

"Mother, we are going to stroll in the gardens."

He slid Faith a sideways glance, taking in her pallor and the brackets framing her pretty mouth that turned upward in a valiant smile. She was brave and possessed fortitude, but he already knew that about her.

He bathed the room with a meaningful glance, taking satisfaction when guests caught staring swiftly averted their attention. "Faith and I would both benefit from a spot of fresh air."

And a break from the pointed stares and discourteous whispers.

Earlier, he'd overheard Lord and Lady Hollister, unaware he stood behind them, as Faith had walked past with Edyth and Charlotte. With a superior sniff, her ladyship had declared to her husband, "That gel will *never* be a proper lady."

It had taken all his self-restraint not to remind the haughty dame that her origins were less than prestigious.

By thunder, Constantine hadn't expected such overt censure of his selection of a bride.

Not that Faith *was* his choice, but the guests presuming to take offense didn't know that. Besides, it wasn't as if he was the ducal heir, blast it, and was expected to marry a high-ranking woman.

How dare they object?

Because Faith wasn't a blueblood?

A spoiled, indulged and pampered, selfish aristocrat?

Hold there, old man. Your sisters aren't any of those things.

That was true.

How did anyone besides the immediate family and Harvey know Faith's origins anyway?

Mayhap they didn't. Perhaps, Constantine was jumping to conclusions, or his guilt over the subterfuge made him suspicious and paranoid. Qualities he disliked in others and positively loathed in himself.

To be fair, he and Faith had received several sincere felicitations as well.

She'd responded with reserved graciousness.

How well Constantine knew how much she despised the artifice. His forearm had suffered her nails digging into the flesh several times while she courteously responded. As his coat and shirt protected his flesh, no actual damage had been inflicted.

The warm congratulations made Constantine's conscience wince with guilt and placed him squarely in the category of cad and bounder. Deception wasn't something he enjoyed.

Unlike Cedric—if his brother truly was a covert operative

—Constantine would've made a lousy spy. All that subterfuge and lying were beyond him. Even as a child, he'd been a horrid liar and always confessed his misdeeds. It took a special person to live a life of deceit for a righteous cause.

An appalling thought struck him mute and stalled his heart for a beat.

Fiend seize it.

Wasn't that *exactly* what *he* was doing?

Lying about his betrothal to protect Charlotte, Edyth, and the rest of the family?

"An excellent notion." Mother beamed with approval, a conspiratorial sheen in her eyes. Likely, she thought he and Faith were doing their part to make the charade believable.

"What?"

His thoughts elsewhere, Constantine stared at her blankly for a moment before she veered her gaze to the veranda in a pointed message.

The merest titter escaped Faith before she wrestled it under control and schooled her features. Nevertheless, hilarity twinkled in her big brown eyes.

The little wretch. Finding amusement at his expense.

Nonetheless, his lips trembled in response to her merriment.

"Just the thing," Mother said, giving him a look that suggested he was as simple-minded as a cabbage. "Seek a bit of privacy from the crowd *outdoors*."

Oh, yes, the walk.

Another muffled giggle echoed from Faith, and a slow, speculative smile wreathed Mother's face.

"We're not..." Constantine checked his objection as Martin slithered close.

"Aunt Mabel, I vow you look younger every time I see

you. You must share your beauty secrets with Tabitha and Ramona. They could use the advice."

His oily smile was as insincere as the sycophantic compliment. His focus shifted to Faith, and he did not attempt to hide the male interest darkening his gray eyes to charcoal.

The rotten blighter.

Daring to ogle another man's—*his cousin's*—fiancé.

Had his impudence no limits?

Constantine curled his free hand into a fist, or else he'd wipe the smug expression from his cousin's face with his knuckles. Normally, he reserved fisticuffs for the ring, but in Martin's case, he could make an exception.

However, instead of pummeling Martin to next Christmastide, Constantine speared him with a murderous glare that held a promise.

Leave off now, or you'll regret it, you sodding reprobate.

Anything but stupid, Martin smirked but heeded the unspoken threat by shifting his focus back to Mother.

Constantine hadn't had a chance to warn Faith about Martin. He would do so as soon as they set foot outdoors. Martin was a notorious libertine. A rakehell and rabble-rouser. No woman, from fresh-from-the-schoolroom innocent to experienced demimonde, was immune to his lascivious pursuit.

"With our mother gone these many years, my sisters have no one to teach them about such things," Martin said while eyeing Miss Breadalbane, who simpered coyly under his regard.

Pure rubbish.

Uncle Hayward doted on his daughters. Nothing was too good, expensive, or impractical for Tabitha and Ramona. Which partially explained why Uncle lived on credit these past few years if the rumors were true.

Fourteen years his junior, Martin had not welcomed his twin sisters with open arms. Until their unexpected arrival, he'd been a spoiled and cosseted only child. One and forty when she delivered the twins and weakened by their birth, Aunt Nora had died a month before their first birthday.

Martin had never forgiven his sisters for their mother's death—he'd been Aunt Nora's favorite—or for the attention Uncle Hayward bestowed upon the twins, who he clearly favored over his irascible son.

Martin's jealousy continued to this day, and not just toward his sisters.

It irked him to no end that his father hadn't been born first and wasn't the duke, thereby making Martin the next in line to inherit the duchy.

Mother gave her nephew a tolerant, if somewhat stiff, smile.

"Your sisters don't need any help from me, Martin. They are lovely in their own right."

Outwardly.

Inwardly...?

That was a wholly different story.

Featherbrained, vain, and incapable of cobbling an intelligent sentence together, they were the sort of chits who gave debutantes a poor name.

Having had enough of his cousin's superior airs, Constantine shifted to guide Faith from the room. "Please excuse us."

Boorish clod that he was, Martin ignored the obvious attempt to escape his company.

"Miss Roth, you never did say how you and Constantine became acquainted." There was that sly upward sweep of Martin's mouth again. "I feel certain it's a romantic tale."

As was her habit, Faith met his gaze directly.

"Tut, tut, Mr. Kellinggrave." She shook her head and wagged a finger at him in mock chastisement. "Fishing for details when I've already told you that Constantine and I are not discussing our betrothal. This house party and these guests"—she swept the room with her gaze—"are here for Lady Charlotte and Mr. Howerton. I refuse to steal their thunder."

Constantine couldn't contain his delighted chuckle. She'd taken Martin down a peg, and very neatly too.

"As you say." His features tense with irritation, Martin bowed and departed without another word.

"That, my dear Miss Roth, was very well done of you."

Approval shone in Mother's eyes.

Faith had won the duchess over. No easy task.

"Thank you, Your Grace. I but spoke the truth."

"Go on with you." Mother made a shooing motion. "Have your walk. Mrs. Shufflebottom is about to descend upon us, and if you do not flee now, you may not be able to. She's impossible to escape once she launches into one of her long-winded monologues about her dachshunds' eating and sleeping habits."

Constantine followed his mother's gaze.

Indeed, Mrs. Shufflebottom, wearing a puce gown besieged with ruffles and lace and no fewer than six ostrich feathers poking from what was obviously a wig, cruised forth like a schooner in full sail.

"Oh dear." Mirth crinkled the corners of Faith's eyes. "We cannot have that. Let's be away then."

She stunned Constantine by taking his hand and pulling him toward the open terrace doors. Even with the French windows open, the room had grown warm.

Aware of the inquisitive gazes following their progress, he pasted a besotted grin upon his countenance and matched her pace. Faith had fallen into the role of adoring fiancé with remarkable ease for someone so opposed to the faux betrothal.

And he, a scientist known to be preoccupied and aloof, mightn't ever regain his taciturn reputation. What was more, at the moment, as he followed the slender woman who had disrupted his life in so many ways from the room, he didn't bloody well care.

And that scared the absolute spit out of him.

TEN

I probably shouldn't put this to pen, lest someone find out, but who would open my correspondences? Through no fault of my own, I'm in the most impossible position. I shan't go into all the details on paper, but dire circumstances have forced Lord Constantine Kellinggrave and me to pretend to be betrothed until the house party for his sister's wedding is over.

This might be the ruin of me and my career as a scrivener. Then what shall I do?

I fear teaching is beyond my scope of patience, although I might manage as a companion.

~Miss Faith Roth, in a letter
to Mrs. Purity Mayfield
Penned while waiting in Lady Edyth's bedchamber

Dovetonwick Court gardens

"Are you certain we should be out here, Constantine?"

Even though society deemed it perfectly acceptable for an affianced couple to take a turn about the gardens unchaperoned, Faith couldn't help but feel scandalous. Because she knew the truth and that those facts were scandal worthy.

"I'm not certain of anything, Faith, but we both needed a reprieve. The gardens and grounds are the only places we'll find a bit of tranquility."

Constantine guided them to the garden's farthest side along a winding gravel path with practiced ease. Edged in fragrant purple and pink hydrangeas with rows of vibrant lilies in shades she'd never seen before nestled amongst various shades of pink phlox in front, the color scheme was breathtaking.

She'd always been partial to pink, though, with her hair, she avoided wearing the color.

Stopping, Faith bent to sniff a lily, taking care not to get the yellow pollen on her nose.

"Isn't it late in the season for them to be blooming?" She gestured to the bed before which they stood, then glanced around them. Numerous plants were still pregnant with buds and blooms. "Most gardens have faded by now."

Leaning a shoulder against a flowering plum tree, Constantine crossed his arms, causing the fabric to stretch taut. Not that Faith made a point of noticing such details about her employer, but really.

How could she *not* notice?

She had eyes.

"Mother's head gardener is a genius at coaxing a few more blossoms from plants. He says it's the fish he works in around the roots."

Constantine gave her a lazy grin, and the oddest thing happened to Faith's knees.

The silly appendages unexpectedly went jelly-like for a heartbeat or two.

Since when did she, Faith Stephanie Hannah Shephard Roth, who had no more notion of how to flirt, bat her eyelashes, or behave coyly, react like an empty-headed, giggling debutante when a handsome man smiled at her?

Indeed not.

She stiffened her legs, locking her knees.

There.

No more nonsense.

Weak knees, indeed.

Not for sensible, independent women who must make their own way in the world.

A fat bumblebee lazily bobbed past, first inspecting a pink and white lily before floating to a purplish-pink phlox. One last sip of nectar before returning to its hive for the night.

"It's here, amongst these plants, flowers, and trees, where I first became enamored with insects," Constantine said. "Particularly butterflies, and also dragonflies and sometimes even damselflies, though the latter two prefer the area by the pond, east of the mansion."

Faith scrunched her nose as she watched the bumblebee fly away. "I thought dragonflies were the males and damselflies the females."

"No, though they are of the same species, Odonata."

Looking over her head, a slight frown pulled his eyebrows together.

She followed his gaze.

Martin Kellinggrave, an older gentleman, and two young ladies stood at the top of the terrace steps.

"Your uncle, Ramona, and Tabitha, I presume?"

Faith sniffed another lily. They'd always been a favorite of hers.

"Indeed." He extended his hand. "Come. I know a secluded garden that the guests don't have access to. This time of evening, it should be lovely, if a bit shadowy."

Cutting a glance at the mansion from beneath her lashes, Faith bit her lip.

She didn't want to return to the house. Nor did she relish another encounter with Martin. But to venture to an area of the gardens alone with Constantine...

Don't be a ninny. A goose. A twiddlepoop.

You've been alone with him dozens of times while working.

Yes, but that was before she became aware of him as a virile, attractive man.

Before close to one hundred people had been led to believe he would be her husband.

"Faith?"

Kindness crinkled his eyes at the corners. Hadn't she believed him incapable of kindness mere days ago?

"I understand your reluctance. This farce is quite trying to you."

For him too. He'd not wanted to participate any more than Faith had.

"I sometimes forget that. Forgive me." He began lowering his hand.

His empathy was Faith's undoing, and her resolve to remain impervious to Lord Constantine Kellinggrave floated away like dandelion down on a summer's breeze.

Until arriving at Dovetonwick Court, they'd constantly butted heads, each mulishly determined to outwit the other and emerge the victor. Not exactly enemies, but certainly not friends, but this new role as an affianced couple thrust them into an awkward alliance.

"No. I want to." Faith clasped his hand and stifled a gasp

at the jolt the contact caused to zip up her arm, even through their gloves.

Likely just static electricity.

His grin widened, making him appear younger and more carefree than she'd ever seen him.

"This way."

Running down the trail, her hand cocooned in his much larger palm and the buzz of the guests fading in the distance, Faith could almost believe there was something real and wonderful between this man and her. And for an instant, she longed for that elusive *something* she'd convinced herself she didn't need or want.

Love.

Love of a man like Constantine.

A decent man. An honorable man.

Dependable and honest and kind.

Slightly eccentric, absent-minded, and obsessive too.

Even those traits that had aggravated her a couple of days ago had become endearing.

She should be alarmed at her musings, but Constantine made her want impossible things. Impractical things: To marry and have children and create a home, life, and a future together.

All whimsical fantasies that she'd dismissed as nonsensical and childlike on her fourteenth birthday. Because even at that tender age, she recognized women's limited power and determined she would never be at a man's mercy.

After all, an unknown man had placed her in Haven House and Academy for the Enrichment of Young Women. She knew that much, although she'd never known why. Faith also never indulged in self-pity. To do so was fruitless and prevented one from moving forward.

At least she had a place to live, food in her belly, received an exceptional education, and made lifelong friends due to the many years she'd lived at the school.

Looking behind him, Constantine smiled at her. Such a disarming pleased upward sweep of his mouth that not only did her knees unhinge once more, her heart she'd so resolutely kept sealed and impenetrable unfurled and let him inside.

Yes, rushing off to a secret garden was foolhardy and impetuous, but wasn't she entitled to a little harmless imprudence? Faith had adhered to strictures and expectations all her life, never once stepping beyond the mark. Always abiding by rules and always aware one misstep could spell ruin.

At this moment, she didn't give two farthings.

Very uncharacteristic, and of more importance, a risk she could ill afford to take.

As they approached a weathered, arched wooden gate, Constantine slowed their pace.

"Give me a moment to find the key," he said, slightly out of breath.

Her breathing had become ragged, but the dash through the gardens wasn't entirely to blame for her breathlessness.

He released Faith's hand, and the simple gesture left her somewhat bereft. After poking around the bricks framing the arched gate on either side, he let out a small whoop.

"Here it is." He shot her a mischievous glance over his shoulder. "Only family ever ventures here. It's a private sanctuary for our use only."

"Mayhap I shouldn't trespass then, Constantine. I'm not family."

Shrugging those broad shoulders, he fitted the key in the keyhole.

"For all intents and purposes, at this moment, you are, Faith. In biblical times, a betrothal was as binding as marriage vows."

The smoldering look he gave her ought to have ignited her on the spot. And might've done if his words hadn't given her pause.

Why in the world would he say such a thing?

Neither of them had pledged a troth to the other, and by no means was this fake engagement legally binding.

Good Lord. The very idea.

With a grating scrape of protest, Constantine turned the key in the lock. He placed the key back in its hidey-hole before giving the sturdy steel handle a hefty tug. The gate reluctantly swung open on squeaky hinges, revealing a small paradise.

Constantine stepped aside and, with a flourishing bow, extended his arm. "My lady."

"My lady? Don't you think you're doing it up a bit brown?"

A wry smile bending her mouth, Faith stepped inside and froze. Lips parted and eyes wide, she slowly took in the tableau before her.

"Oh, Constantine. It's the loveliest thing I've ever seen."

Gone were the manicured beds and enthusiastically trimmed bushes and hedges of the formal gardens. This oasis was festooned with blossoms, vines, gnarled trees, at least three bird baths, a waterfall pouring into a large pond in one corner, and a folly strategically placed on a small knoll for the best view. Wisteria vines—the blossoms long since spent—twisted and spiraled around the white marble. When in bloom, the dangling purple blossoms would create a spectacular floral canopy.

So entranced was Faith that she barely registered when the creaky door snicked shut.

Grinning, she pulled off her borrowed gloves. She had every intention of dipping her fingers in the waterfall and mayhap her toes in the pond. Two benches on either side of the pond suggested someone else had the same thought.

Upon closer inspection, Faith realized steps led from the green, blue, and coral mosaic tiles surrounding the pond into the deepest end.

"You can swim in it?" she asked almost breathlessly.

She loved to swim, though opportunities to do so were infrequent.

Not many girls at the academy had enjoyed swimming lessons. Faith had and was an accomplished swimmer. Nevertheless, Mrs. Shepherd had been adamant that learning to swim be a part of their education.

"You never know what skills you may need, my dears. The better prepared you are, the greater your chance of success."

Which was why all of the students at the academy had learned to load and shoot a pistol, had fencing lessons, were instructed in herbal remedies, and were taught rudimentary nursing skills along with traditional lessons in cooking, preserving, sewing, and overseeing a household.

"Indeed." Constantine nodded while gazing about. "My brothers and I did so quite often as youths. Do you swim?"

"I do, although it's been some time since I had the privilege. I imagine your family partakes whenever they have the opportunity."

For certain, Faith would if this were her home.

"I honestly don't know if anyone does anymore, but Le Gardyner ensures our family garden remains in pristine shape."

Faith laughed. "Your gardener's name is Le Gardyner? Really?"

"Aye." Constantine grinned. "He's from a long line of gardeners, hence the appropriate surname. His first name is Oakley." Hands on his slender hips, he shook his head. "I used to swim every time I came home. I'd forgotten how much I enjoy it."

"Me too." Faith ventured closer. The water was clear, cool, and oh so tempting. "I should like to visit during the daytime." She spun around and marched toward one of the wrought iron benches. "I'm going to dip my feet in the water."

"Hold on there." He laughed, reaching out and drawing her near. "You have pollen on your nose."

Even after she'd been so careful?

After removing his handkerchief from his pocket and dipping the corner in the refreshing water, Constantine proceeded to gently wipe the pollen off.

Faith stood utterly still, studying his features mere inches from hers—aware of him in a manner she'd never been before. Conscious of his masculinity and her femininity.

His cologne teased her nostrils, but she also detected his musky, clean personal essence.

"There. No one will mistake you for a pixie or a fairy now."

His gaze meshed with hers, and his smile faded. The look in his eyes became hungry and hot.

He dipped his head nearer, and Faith couldn't tear her attention from his mouth. From lips perfectly formed by a master sculptor.

"Tell me to stop." His voice emerged in a gravelly, low purr. "You've only to say the word."

Stop? Was he insane?

No. No. Go on. *Kiss me. Please kiss me.*

"I don't want you to stop."

Faith wasn't thinking at the moment—didn't want to think. To be logical and sensible and practical and cautious.

What Faith wanted was for Constantine to kiss her. Thoroughly.

She'd never been kissed.

What could one kiss from her pretend fiancé hurt?

Her eyelids fluttered closed of their own volition as he drew her into his marble-like embrace. The first touch was no more than a butterfly's wing.

A whisper. A featherlike touch.

As if realizing her willingness, perhaps even eagerness, Constantine brought his mouth down fully on hers. Such an onslaught of sensation engulfed Faith that she became light-headed, her heart flipped over, and her dashed knees turned to butter.

She clutched his jacket, needing to be closer to him.

The burbling of the waterfall and the songs of the birds dimmed as everything around them faded. It was just Faith and Constantine, tasting, exploring, discovering.

Suddenly, he lifted his head and peered toward the entrance. In the growing twilight, the trees cast dancing shadows in the fairy garden.

"Someone's coming," he whispered.

He swiftly put a respectable distance between them, and once Faith collected her scattered wits, she scrambled to take a seat on the bench on the pond's opposite side.

Thank goodness impending darkness hid her kiss-reddened mouth and flushed cheeks. However, the full moon had crept midway up the sky and would soon bathe the garden in fairy light.

"I thought you said this was a private garden," she whispered, still feeling his hard but also velvety soft mouth upon hers.

"It is." Constantine's focus remained riveted on the gate.

The unmistakable rasping of the key rotating in the lock carried to her ears.

The gate edged inward, and a tall man stepped through the opening.

"Leopold!" Constantine strode across the tile, his shoes clicking a staccato until he reached the grass.

Grinning as broadly as his brother, Leopold met him halfway, and the men embraced.

"Little brother. It's been too long."

He clapped Constantine on the back, his gaze veering to Faith, who'd stood at his entrance.

"This must be your bride-to-be."

Faith found his grin contagious and smiled in return, instantly liking the next Duke of Landrith.

"My warmest felicitations. I had no idea you were courting anyone, Con. Imagine my surprise upon arriving home an hour ago and having no fewer than a dozen guests ask me if I'd met my future sister-in-law yet."

Hadn't the duke or duchess, Lady Charlotte, or Lady Edyth apprised the Marquess of Kenworthy of the facts? Perhaps the family had been occupied, or there hadn't been a moment for a confidential conversation.

"About that, Leo." Constantine pulled his earlobe, appearing almost sheepish. "It's not what it seems, brother."

Faith saw the shadow before Constantine and knew who the interloper was before his vile form stepped into the garden. Ominousness and suspicion shrouded Martin Kellinggrave like the pernicious serpent in the Garden of Eden.

How long had he been listening?

He examined the brothers with a shrewdness that bordered on eerie before his reptilian gaze caressed Faith.

She shuddered but resisted the impulse to cross her arms in a protective gesture. By all that was holy, she would not let the lecher see her disquiet. He probably enjoyed unnerving women.

"What is not what it seems?" Martin asked.

ELEVEN

I seek an intelligent, well-read, independent young woman of good breeding. A lady of substance who isn't afraid of getting her hands dirty, and doesn't swoon or fly into hysterics when encountering an insect, a bat, or a wild animal. She must be an excellent scribe, capable of making a decent cup of tea, and willing to live in less than luxurious conditions while on expeditions.

Acceptable candidates must be able to swim and ride proficiently and endure lengthy coach travel. The capacity to handle a firearm or a blade is a bonus, as is the ability to sew and cook as needed. Basic nursing skills are desired but not required. The ideal candidate won't object to traveling for months or perhaps years without returning to England.

~Mrs. Eustasia Peagilly in an advert
placed in *The Times* for a companion

Bollocks.

The last thing Constantine needed was for Martin to become suspicious about the betrothal. His cousin would like nothing better than to see this branch of the Kellinggrave's immersed in a scandal—no matter how inconsequential.

One would think a man with Martin's sordid reputation wouldn't be altogether keen to point a judgmental finger. But wasn't that the way of people? Eager to point out the speck of sawdust in someone else's eye while ignoring the plank in their own.

Leopold swiveled to face Martin and gave him a terse nod. "Martin."

Palpable tension radiated between the cousins, and all the while, the waterfall serenely cascaded into the pond with a soft whoosh, oblivious to the disharmony that had invaded the sanctuary.

Too bad Martin couldn't have been cut from the guest list. The house party would be more enjoyable for all and safer for the women.

"Ah, the adored heir has returned to his family's loving embrace at last. Six months is rather neglectful of you, cuz." Grasping his lapel, Martin cocked his head, a snide half-smile quirking his mouth. "Sowing your wild oats before you're forced to settle down and take on your ducal responsibilities, eh?"

Malice dripped from every acerbic word.

Already obscenely jealous, Martin's obsession with the dukedom bordered on unbalanced. Would he never move on and let the matter go?

He hadn't been cheated or robbed.

No one had conspired to steal his birthright.

Chance, providence, destiny, or perhaps the Lord himself had decreed that Father be born first, and that same divine power had gifted him three sons. An heir and two spares. Uncle Hayward had accepted his lot in life, and if not with graciousness, at least he wasn't a sulky pout, unlike his son.

Expression inscrutable except for the coldness in the wintery gaze he speared their cousin, Leopold put a few feet between himself and Martin. Probably so he didn't pummel the obnoxious sod into next month.

"Thankfully, as Father is hearty and hale, I needn't concern myself with such morose contemplations, need I?" His scrutiny scathing, Leopold rested a hand on his hip. "You really oughtn't to either, Martin. Bad form and all of that. One *might* think you wish ill upon the current Duke of Landrith."

Constantine hid a grin at the deliberate jab.

Martin didn't deny the accusation, but his hostile glare spoke for him.

He'd very much like Father, Leopold, Cedric, Constantine, and even Uncle Hayward to kick up their toes, clearing an unobstructed pathway for Martin to inherit the duchy.

What caused a person to be inherently vile?

Stilted silence descended upon the garden, as gloomy and unwelcome as a death shroud.

Faith skirted the bench and, offering Leopold a brilliant smile, dipped into a pretty curtsy.

"My lord. I would love to hear about your travels. I've always longed to see the world. Lady Edyth tells me you've recently visited Egypt. Was it wondrous?"

Faith wanted to travel?

Even with her penchant for becoming queasy in a coach?

Why hadn't Constantine known that?

Truth be told, he knew scant little about her, particularly her hopes and dreams. But then, when would the subject have come up? And was it really wise to learn more?

No.

Neither had that kiss been prudent, and it must not be repeated.

Constantine had no logical excuse for kissing Faith. He attributed it to the garden's romantic atmosphere. What else could have addled him to the point of rashness?

He was not an impulsive fellow.

Most of the time, Faith vexed him like no other.

Even now, he had serious doubts about continuing her employment, ridiculous wager aside. Though while he'd have gladly seen the back of her head a week ago, the thought of never seeing her again after this week cramped his gut.

Mayhap the fish had been off, for surely he wasn't feeling sentimental.

"Indeed, Miss Roth. Egypt was majestic and marvelous." A tanner, thicker version of Constantine with slightly darker hair, Leopold offered her his elbow. "Permit me to accompany you to the house, and I shall regale you with stories about the pyramids. I toured a tomb while there. I hoped to see a mummy but wasn't that fortunate."

Martin muttered sourly, "It's unnatural to desecrate a body in such a manner."

"Oh, but it's utterly fascinating." She cast Constantine a mischievous glance from the corner of her eye.

Yes, little vixen. I know what you did.

Faith had neatly changed the subject and left Martin's intrusive question unanswered.

Constantine gave her a conspiratorial wink, and her eyes rounded the merest bit.

Martin fairly fumed with suppressed irritation.

He'd not let the matter go. Of that, Constantine was certain. Which meant he needed to warn Mother and the others to speak most carefully when Martin prowled about.

Everyone should give him a wide berth, as one would a venomous spider or poisonous snake.

"Let's return to the house, shall we?" Constantine addressed Martin. "Mother mentioned she'd scheduled musical entertainment for after supper."

"Probably some tone-deaf chit with a voice like a dying crow." Martin perused the peaceful garden. "No, thank you. I'll pass on the auditory torture. I'd prefer to remain here for a while."

Leopold turned back at the entrance and glared. "No."

He didn't soften his refusal with a platitude or explanation. Instead, he reached inside his coat and removed the key. He extended it toward Constantine.

"Make sure to lock the gate, won't you?"

Martin knew the garden was for the immediate family's use. He'd been invited inside a few times growing up. However, he'd been banished after maliciously destroying several planters, dumping the remnants in the pond, and painting obscenities on the stone walls.

As Constantine accepted the heavy iron key, he made a mental note to find a new hiding place.

"As you wish," Martin said in a tone that was anything but deferential. With a contemptuous glance around the oasis, he shrugged. "I need a brandy in any event."

Constantine waited until Martin preceded him from the garden before he shut the gate and locked it. After dropping the key into a pocket inside his jacket, he clasped his hands behind his back and followed the others toward the house.

The moonlight from the clear sky strewn with millions and millions of twinkling diamond-like stars provided ample light for their return. In the distance, the gardens' lanterns glowed invitingly. Voices, laughter, and music floated across the warm honeysuckle-scented air.

In a few short weeks, autumn would descend upon the countryside, dramatically changing the landscape. Constantine had always preferred summers to the cold and damp of winter. Mayhap he ought to try a bit of traveling to warm climes himself. He could further his studies of butterflies and moths in exotic locations. It might be quite fascinating, in truth.

Leopold drew to a halt a few feet from the base of the stairs leading to the terrace. Two older couples strolled past, trailed by a trio of young women. One skimmed her gaze over Leopold and Faith before leaning in to hear what her companion said.

Martin stomped by them without a word.

Surly blighter.

"I'll return you to your betrothed, Miss Roth." Leopold swept his overlong hair off his forehead. "It may be premature of me, but I think you will be a wonderful addition to the family."

"Thank you." Faith withdrew her hand from his elbow and raised guilt-filled eyes to Constantine's. "If you'll excuse me, I would like to visit the retiring room."

"Of course." Leo bent into a chivalrous bow, putting his notorious charm on full display.

Few women could resist Leopold when he decided to play the gallant. Faith, however, seemed impervious to his charm, for which Constantine was far gladder than logic could explain.

A frown tugging his eyebrows together, he observed her hasty departure.

Grasping her skirts in one hand, she nimbly climbed the stairs, the lanterns' glow casting ribbons of fire in her hair. Face slightly pinched, she looked neither to the left nor the right but made straight for the French windows.

"Leo?" After a swift glance around to ensure no one overheard him, Constantine stepped nearer and murmured, "Miss Roth and I aren't really betrothed."

Chuckling, Leo threw an arm across Constantine's shoulders.

"I know, Con. But for the benefit of the guests yonder"—he jabbed his thumb over his shoulder—"and our least favorite cousin, whom I spied lurking in the shrubberies outside the garden, eavesdropping on you and Miss Roth, I played along."

Of course, Martin would spy on Constantine and Faith, the miscreant. "He better direct his snooping elsewhere, or I'll be obliged to realign his nose."

"You'd be doing him a favor." Leopold skewed his mouth sideways. "I vow, every time I see Martin, he's become more offensive, though I cannot conceive how that is possible."

Constantine nodded as he fell into step beside his brother. "It may be time for Mother and Father to put aside familial loyalty and shun him like the miserable bounder he is."

"That will make him even more resentful and spiteful, but I believe you are right." Leopold rubbed his chin. "I don't trust him."

"Neither do I." Constantine smiled at Howerton and Charlotte as they strolled the terrace, eyes only for each other. "His coveting the duchy has reached an unhealthy fixation. I intend to have a word with Father regarding my concerns."

Leo waggled his eyebrows. "What say you, we raid Father's best Scotch like we used to, Con?"

He'd always been the incorrigible brother.

"I wouldn't mind a finger's worth," Constantine conceded, changing directions and striding away from the milling guests. Paralleling the terrace, Constantine and his brother headed for the study.

"I like your Miss Roth, nevertheless. She's smart and

capable of actually conversing." Leopold elbowed Constantine in the side, giving him a teasing grin. "Is she *really* your scrivener? I'd love to hear how that came about."

"Shh," Constantine warned, with an apprehensive glance around.

No one was near enough to hear Leopold, but still. One could never be too careful. In truth, Constantine should never have permitted this ruse. Lies always required more lies. He feared the repercussions from this betrothal farce might be far worse than the initial gossip.

And Faith was the person with the most to lose.

"I'll tell you, Leo, but when we're assured of privacy."

In short order, they slipped inside the study through a side door. The draperies had been drawn, and no fire crackled in the hearth. A turned-down brass oil lamp with a hand-painted globe shade burned low on a mahogany table in the center of the room, casting shadows into the dim corners.

Leopold puffed out a loud sigh as he lifted the stopper from the cut crystal decanter.

"Mother says there will be close to a hundred guests staying the week, and at least another hundred are expected for the ball."

"That many?" Constantine rested his hip on the edge of the desk.

All the more trying for Faith.

Had it only been last night that he'd penned the short note to her in this room, basically asking her to be a cooperative prisoner?

"Aye." Grimacing, Leo poured a dram into two tumblers. He glanced up through hooded eyelids. "That is why I stay away. I cannot abide these crowds. All of the falderol and posturing."

What Leopold couldn't abide was the gaggle of women he

attracted—like moths to the proverbial flame—each hoping she might catch his eye and become his bride. Each coveting the position of Duchess of Landrith.

"You could invent a faux betrothed too," Constantine quipped, accepting the glass his brother extended. "Claim your affianced is somewhere on the other side of England or, better yet, out of the country. Then you'd be free to enjoy yourself."

Leo took a swallow, and Constantine did the same. The liquor burned a path to his belly. Unlike most of polite society, he rarely imbibed in spirits stronger than wine. And most especially, he hadn't since the debacle where he'd stupidly bet he would hire a female amanuensis. Just to prove he wasn't a stodgy, antiquated boor.

An ironic smile teased the corners of his mouth.

What would those friends say to learn he was involved in a fake betrothal?

"Hmm, I might very well consider it." Leo slid Constantine a teasing glance. "Too bad the only woman who might pass muster is already spoken for. It wouldn't do for me to steal my little brother's affianced. Imagine *that* scandal!"

Unfamiliar jealousy spiraled around Constantine's middle, but he tamped down the ugly emotion. This was his brother, for God's sake. No woman would ever come between them. Besides, Leo but jested.

"Trust me when I say that is not a path you want to venture down, Leo. I rue the day I met the mulish, opinionated termagant."

"Termagant, you say? Miss Roth seemed the epitome of a mild-mannered, temperate, and decorous young woman." Hilarity leeched into Leo's voice. "I think though doth protest too much, brother."

Constantine snorted. "You wouldn't say that if you knew her."

He should have left off insulting Faith there. She didn't deserve his disdain nor being besmirched to Leo, but some unnameable devil urged Constantine onward.

"Faith Roth has been a constant, irritating thorn in my backside, and I have been trying to rid myself of her since I hired her. Then as bad luck would have it, I must now act the lovesick fool and pretend she is my betrothed."

A quickly stifled but unmistakable gasp filtered from behind the draperies.

"Who's there?" Leopold set his glass down before striding across the room and yanking back the burgundy brocade panel.

Devil take it.

Faith stood there, one hand pressed to her chest and the other to her mouth. Pale as cream, she trembled slightly like a frightened butterfly. But it was her big wounded brown eyes staring across the room at Constantine that stabbed him as sharply and deeply as a blade to his heart.

God, what have I done?

He hadn't meant a word of it.

Not a single syllable.

He'd simply wanted to discourage Leo's budding interest and, even more, his own growing fascination. She was not for him. They were too different and rubbed each other the wrong way.

Not when you kissed her.

Faith slowly lowered her hands, balling them into fists. Her chest rose and fell with shallow breaths, humiliation fairly oozing from her. Her composure under the circumstances was estimable.

She spared Leopold an apologetic glance.

Her voice a mere wisp of sound, she said, "I dashed in here to hide. I thought I saw someone I knew who would know I wasn't betrothed. I honestly didn't mean to intrude or eavesdrop."

Who did she know?

Why hide from them?

"I don't doubt it." Leo angled his head, sadness darkening his eyes as he looked between Faith and Constantine. A tinge of rebuke entered his gaze, making Constantine feel all the more the cad for his careless, caustic words. "I shall permit you some privacy."

"No need, my lord." Faith thrust out that stubborn chin as Constantine had seen her do dozens of times. Only this time, sparks of betrayal and chagrin spewed from the fire crackling in her eyes.

Nevertheless, Leo slipped from the room, but not before giving Constantine another half-pitying, half-condemning look which all but shouted, *"Not well done of you."*

The former he despised. The latter he deserved, but it was paltry compared to the self-castigation tunneling through his blood, leaving a scalding path of remorse.

Faith stared somewhere past Constantine's shoulder as if she couldn't bear to look upon him.

"I tender my resignation, Lord Constantine, effective immediately. I also refuse to continue this charade of a betrothal."

He'd expected both, yet an objection throttled to his throat.

"Faith...forgive me."

Constantine took two steps toward her, but her expression brought him up short. He'd seen her miffed, peeved, outraged, amused, shocked, and angry. But never had he seen the utter devastation ravaging her winsome features. And *he'd* caused that pain.

The knife twisted again, deeper still.

"Please, let me explain."

How could he?

I'm an assling. A bounder. A selfish shallow blackguard.

I was afraid of what I am beginning to feel for you.

"Don't you dare try to placate me." Faith's voice shook with outrage, yet she never raised the pitch. "I intend to leave this house tonight. I hope that you will at least do me the courtesy of paying me my wages. You can leave them with the butler because I never wish to see or speak to you again after this."

Never see her again?

A freight wagon slamming into Constantine or being trampled by stampeding horses would've hurt less.

No. No.

I must make this right. Somehow, I must.

"Faith, you don't have to leave."

I don't want you to leave.

Constantine closed the distance between them and reached to touch her shoulder, but at the seething glance she cut him, he let his hand drop to his side.

"Oh, but *I* do. I do not stay where I am ridiculed and disparaged. *I* did not place the ridiculous bet that led you to hire me. Despite haranguing me daily and making it clear that you wanted me to quit, I performed my duties with diligence and professionalism."

She took a step closer and poked him in the chest. Hard.

"Nevertheless, I endured your rudeness and hostility because, unlike you, I *have* to work...to make my own way in the world because I don't have family or finances, Lord Constantine."

She spat his name as if it was offal, and she couldn't bear the taste on her tongue.

So pale now, he feared she might swoon, Faith sucked in a ragged breath.

But Miss Faith Roth would never concede such a weakness in his presence.

She marched toward the door, the muted light smudging her dear features. Her voice, however, was crisp and clear, snapping with anger and hurt.

"I'll remind you that I did you and your family a colossal favor, going against my better judgment, my conscience, and compromising my integrity. I would've seen that betrothal farce to the end, but as you have so succinctly and vehemently expressed, you cannot abide my presence. I feel no obligation to continue. I shall allow you to explain why to the others."

She opened the door and, after checking the passageway, stepped into the corridor. "I shan't say farewell as you've made it abundantly clear I've never been anything but an annoying pebble in your shoe."

"Faith...please."

Constantine couldn't breathe. A tidal wave of guilt and desolation was drowning him.

He couldn't let her go. Not like this. Not with her believing those ugly things he'd said.

Then why did you say them, you buffleheaded codpiece?

Because he didn't want Leo to find her attractive.

Idiot. Dolt. Imbecile.

"You are an ungrateful, arrogant, narrow-minded...." The tears pooling in her beautiful eyes spilled over, and she spun around and darted away.

He'd made her cry.

Valiant, brave, remarkable, incomparable Faith.

Fiend seize it. What have I done?

Ramona's high-pitched voice scraped across the silence.

"I do believe the little nobody tossed Con over, Tabitha."

TWELVE

I am delighted to inform you that I shall be able to attend your soirée. My new employer has agreed to give me a half day off, only because her niece will be in town for a short visit. It's quite a concession for Mrs. Templemore, I assure you, but still, I am grateful. It's been ever so long since I've seen my friends except unexpectedly seeing Purity at a house party recently.

For one accustomed to traveling worldwide for several years, remaining in England for any period is a blessing. Although I'm not positive if given the opportunity to act as a companion for a world traveler again, I would not seize it. How else does a woman of my station visit so many enthralling places and see so many awe-inspiring sights?

~Miss Trinity Ablethorne, in a brief note
to Mrs. Joy Morrisette

Dovetonwick Court upper story

Ten minutes later

Head down and face averted, Faith made straight for Lady Edyth's bedchamber. Not an easy task with a house swarming with guests, made worse by her atrocious sense of direction. That was the main reason she daren't walk to the village tonight. She'd become lost for certain.

The whole while Faith negotiated the various corridors and passages, she prayed she wouldn't encounter anyone and have to offer an explanation for her reddened eyes and why she wasn't enjoying the festivities or hanging on the arm of her *betrothed.*

Former fake betrothed.

I rue the day I ever met the mulish, opinionated termagant.

Constantine's spiteful words replayed in her head, a cruel mantra of her failings.

How stupid of her to have thought they'd turned a corner in their relationship—that they might become friends or... Perhaps something more.

She hadn't examined what the *more* might entail. No sense putting the cart before the horse and all that. Since when did she, pragmatic and practical Faith Roth, entertain fanciful daydreams?

Twice on her solitary sojourn to Lady Edyth's bedchamber, Faith made wrong turns and had to retrace her steps. Once, her heart thudding like a kettle drum between her ears, she'd dived behind a curtained alcove and held her breath when she heard men's voices in the distance. She feared the Kellinggraves had come in search of her, and she was not prepared to face any of the family just yet.

Thankfully, her crying stint had been short-lived. Not only wasn't she a hen-hearted weeper or the self-pitying sort by nature, but Faith also refused to allow Lord Constantine that control over her. Her initial despair and chagrin had transformed into justified, fulminating anger. That anger fueled her resolve to be away from Dovetonwick Court tonight—wisdom be hanged.

That he could speak of her so disparagingly after they'd shared that marvelous kiss in the gardens. Well, that clearly indicated the kiss meant far more to her than him.

And why shouldn't it?

He was a man of the world, after all. Rich, handsome, privileged. He probably kissed women all of the time. Pretty, perfumed, creamy-skinned women who whispered how much they adored him, and not commoners with ink-stained fingers and a smattering of freckles across their nose.

Bah.

So what if it had been Faith's first kiss?

Those were always memorable.

Weren't they?

That was the only reason she'd found his firm lips upon hers special. There would be other kisses.

Mayhap.

Faith hadn't quite planned how to depart the premises without alerting the duke and duchess. They'd try to talk her out of leaving. At least the duchess would.

Faith felt sure of it.

She couldn't very well order a coach brought 'round, *could* she?

And she'd gargle hot coals before she asked to use Constantine's conveyance.

She intended to stay at a lodging house in the village tonight, and tomorrow, she'd buy a ticket to London on the mail coach. That was if Constantine paid her wages owed.

Surely after his contemptible behavior, he'd not begrudge Faith her wages.

He might very well do so to force her to stay and play out the reprehensible charade. The one thing she despised more than lying was being manipulated. The Kellinggraves had forced her to subject herself to both, and it stirred resentment.

And that caused remorse because Faith wasn't by nature a bitter or unforgiving person.

She caught her lower lip between her teeth.

She'd not brought enough funds with her for a room at an inn or a ticket to London, leaving her in a deuced bumble-broth. She must be away tonight. Her pride would not permit her to stay after what she'd overheard in the study.

Mulish. Termagant. Thorn. Rid of her.

Fresh mortification cleaved her.

How could she ever look Lord Kenworthy in the eye again?

Hot tears sprang to her eyes again as she marched down the corridor, one ear cocked for the sounds of footfalls or voices.

Constantine held her in such contempt. She'd never been anything but an unwanted, irksome burden.

That knowledge shouldn't hurt as profusely as it did.

The game was up in any event, for she was almost certain she'd seen Mercy Brockman. Mercy would never believe Faith had become affianced to Lord Constantine Kellinggrave since they'd last written each other. Nor would Mercy lie about a fake betrothal.

That was the problem with telling tarradiddles.

One led to another, and then to another, until the facts and lies became so tangled that it was nearly impossible to remember what was truth and what was fabricated.

A tear trickled down her cheek, and she angrily swiped at it. Waterworks never achieved anything except for a red, stuffy nose and swollen eyes.

Regardless, two more intrepid droplets dared to follow the first.

Ooh...botheration.

Faith came very near to uttering a most unladylike oath.

How much farther to Lady Edyth's chamber, for pity's sake?

Had she taken another wrong turn?

"Rotten bounder."

If only Constantine really were a rotten bounder.

"Oh, my dear. What has you distraught?"

Faith snapped her head up to discover Mrs. Peagilly standing inside the doorframe to her chamber. She must've either only arrived or was just leaving her chamber.

"I..." Faith swallowed and darted a panicked gaze behind her. "I..."

The dashed words wouldn't form.

Faith blinked frantically as more stinging tears blinded her.

I shall not cry.

"*Tut, tut.* You poor thing." Mrs. Peagilly swept to her side and put an arm about Faith's waist. "Why don't you join an old woman in a soothing cup of tea? Tea always works wonders to calm me when I'm overwrought. And I just happen to have had a fresh pot sent up moments ago."

Before Faith realized what Mrs. Peagilly was about, amid a cloud of violet and lavender perfume, she'd been ushered into the chamber, gently pushed into an overstuffed floral armchair, and a cup of steaming tea had been pressed into her hands.

As Mrs. Peagilly stirred milk and sugar into her cup, she considered Faith. Her modest but elegant midnight blue and ebony gown, the single row of pearls at her throat, and drop pearl earrings dangling from her earlobes bespoke superb taste and quality but a preference for simplicity rather than ostentatiousness.

A woman after Faith's own heart.

"You're not like most other chits, Miss Roth. You have a brain in your head. I see the intelligence in your eyes."

She lifted her pink rose chintz cup from its saucer, her faded blue eyes twinkling over the rim.

"You remind me of me when I was your age, Miss Roth."

That took Faith by surprise. "I do?"

"Indeed. A woman who knows her own mind, isn't afraid of a challenge, and possesses gumption and fortitude that others often find off-putting."

Yes, that did sound very much like Faith.

The dame settled back into the twin to Faith's armchair. Mrs. Peagilly might not be in the first sprig of youth, but her gaze and mind were sharp, and she moved with surprising agility and vigor for a woman her age.

"Charlotte, the sweet dear, apprised me of the truth regarding you and Lord Constantine." She chuckled, not the least abashed. "I might've prodded a bit—very well, a lot. I have a nose for such things." She touched her reedy nose. "I sensed something wasn't quite as it should be between you and Lord Constantine."

"Oh."

What did Faith say to that?

Her initial doubts that she and Lord Constantine could portray a loving couple had proved spot on. How many others had deduced the truth as well? A man who disliked her as much as he did would be hard put not to reveal his real feelings, despite his superb acting abilities.

The kiss sure seemed authentic, the opportunistic bounder.

And did she put up any resistance?

No.

She'd participated like a Covent Garden harlot.

Another wave of chagrin heated her cheeks.

Did this dear lady think less of Faith because of her part in the debacle?

Faith set her cup aside. "I only agreed to the ruse because I didn't want Lady Charlotte's wedding ruined."

And because Faith loathed gossip.

"Very commendable of you." Cocking her silvery head in a manner that reminded Faith of the curious sparrow that perched on the windowsill of her rented room, Mrs. Peagilly said, "I'm a good listener, Miss Roth. Of more importance, I don't bear tales or divulge confidences."

THIRTEEN

I feel certain you know Bernadette's whereabouts, or at the very least, her destination when she left your institution. After all, do you not make every effort to place your charges in respectable positions when they are of a certain age?

Your failure to respond to my last missive tries my patience as my family is eager to reunite with our dear one. Should I not hear from you in a timely fashion, expect a private investigator to call upon you within a fortnight.

By the by, what name does Bernadette go by now? I am aware it is standard practice for you to rename each child to protect the privacy and confidentiality of the parties involved.

~Mr. Aloysius Petheringham, in a
terse letter to Mrs. Hester Shepherd

Still in Mrs. Peagilly's sitting room
Six tick-tocks of the inlaid mahogany bracket clock later

Faith hadn't intended to unburden herself, but it had been so long since she'd confided in anyone that the sordid details spilled forth. At first stilted and awkward, then with increasing ease.

"Here, my dear."

She accepted the lacy bit of cloth passing for a handkerchief that Mrs. Peagilly handed her.

After drying her eyes and blowing her nose, she gave a rueful laugh.

"Now I'm out of a position and haven't the means to return to London."

Teacup on her lap and tapping the fingertips of one hand on her chair's arm, Mrs. Peagilly peered at Faith, those blue eyes alight with wisdom and discernment. "I think I may have a solution that would benefit us both."

Faith perked up at that. "Have you need of a scribe?"

"Not precisely." Laying aside her teacup, Mrs. Peagilly shook her head. "I seek a traveling companion who can also act as a scrivener. Someone with a backbone and good sense who won't faint dead away if she sees an elephant or a spider."

Elephant? Spider?

Faith couldn't prevent her eyes from going wide.

Mrs. Peagilly really was the most astonishing woman.

"There are great monstrous spiders in other parts of the world. Rather unpleasant creatures with all those black, buggy eyes and hairy legs. But if you leave them alone, for the most part, they leave you alone."

For the most part?

Her merry blue eyes sparkled. "My companion must also be capable of making a decent cup of tea over an open fire."

Faith's enthusiasm sank to her toes, ensconced in borrowed gold slippers.

Could she make tea over a fire?

In truth, she detested spiders of any size. Large snakes too, but an elephant would be most exciting to see.

"The position sounds remarkable." A dream come true, in fact. What great adventures she would have. "But I fear I become queasy in a coach."

"Hmm." Putting a finger to her cheek, Mrs. Peagilly pressed her lips together. "I warrant you've not spent much time in traveling conveyances, have you?"

Her accurate discernment was unexpected. Still, Faith had thought Mrs. Peagilly would rescind the offer with her next breath.

"No," Faith admitted. "Only my journey to London from where I was raised and then this trip to Dovetonwick Court."

"Ah. Just as I suspected." A pleased smile wreathed Mrs. Peagilly's lined face. "The affliction is much like *mal de mer*—sea sickness. As one becomes accustomed to the motion, nausea goes away. Ginger tea is an excellent remedy in the meanwhile. Trust me, my dear. I used to suffer too. Regardless, my determination to see the world proved a great incentive to overcome the affliction. I think you might find that true too."

A tiny sprout of hope dared to spring forth.

Could this be an answer to her prayer?

"I don't have my references with me, but I could send them to you," Faith said, trying to modulate the hope and enthusiasm in her voice.

You're running away, her conscience accused.

Yes. Yes, I am.

Far better to toddle off to parts unknown as a companion than return to London unemployed. And what explanation could she give a future employer as to why she'd left her position?

I lied about being betrothed to my employer and then quit when he told another how much he reviled me. Nothing there to smudge my character.

Waving her hand in a dismissive gesture, Mrs. Peagilly shook her head. "No need. I'm an excellent judge of character. I think we shall march along well together, Miss Roth. I'm off to the Mediterranean in October. I haven't set a departure date quite yet. I should very much like you to accompany me."

"I..."

To the Mediterranean?

Yes, by heavens. Faith would do it. Put this debacle behind her and Lord Constantine Kellinggrave out of her mind. And her heart.

A silver lining in the gunmetal-gray cloud that had descended upon her life. With a firm nod and grateful smile, she said, "I would be honored to accept your offer, Mrs. Peagilly."

"Excellent." Mrs. Peagilly collected her teacup once more and took a drink. "You shall need to apply for a passport."

"Of course." How did one who had no idea where they were born or who their parents were apply for a passport? Trinity Ablethorne would know. Another foundling, Trinity had traveled extensively.

Faith would write her at once.

"One more thing, Miss Roth...."

Faith put her musings aside and concentrated on Mrs. Peagilly once more. "Yes?"

"I would ask that you remain here until after the wedding," Mrs. Peagilly said gently. "Until the house party officially ends next week, in point of fact."

Oh, dear.

How could Faith face Constantine or the Marquess of Kenworthy again after the humiliation in the study? Mortification left invisible wounds that might scar over in time but would always be a reminder.

Mrs. Peagilly must've seen Faith's hesitation and reluctance.

"It shall give us time to become acquainted." Mrs. Peagilly waved her hand again, and her teacup rattled in the saucer. "As you can see, I've been given a suite. There's a small chamber through that doorway. You can sleep there if you don't wish to remain where you are. I expect the duchess thought I'd bring a lady's maid with me."

She chuckled and poured herself more tea but didn't pick up the cup. "I've been dressing and undressing for decades, as well as styling my own hair. Both are under-appreciated skills."

Faith well knew that. She'd never had a lady's maid.

What orphan had?

She'd have to grit her teeth, bite her tongue, and, whenever possible, avoid Constantine and the rest of the Kellinggraves for three more days. The ball was tomorrow night, the wedding the next day, and she and Mrs. Peagilly could be on their way at dawn's first light the following morn.

Faith would need time to settle her affairs, give up her room at the lodging house, and would still be able to attend Joy Morrissette's soirée and say farewell to her friends.

A gnawing ache behind her ribs took her breath for a moment. She should be happy that she'd never have to lay eyes on Lord Constantine Kellinggrave again. Instead, bone-penetrating sorrow sluiced through her.

Nevertheless, she was encouraged at her new prospects, though not thrilled to have to concede her plan to leave Dovetonwick Court tonight.

Faith impulsively bent and hugged Mrs. Peagilly.

"Thank you. I am most grateful."

Mrs. Peagilly patted her back, then clasped a hand.

"I assure you, my dear, there will be many times you won't thank me. I do not travel the typical tourist routes. However, I can guarantee you'll never be the same. I shall give you a taste of freedom and adventure generally reserved for men."

A steeliness infused Faith's spine as she straightened.

Three more interminable days, and she'd be away from here and employed by someone who actually wanted her to work for them. A weight lifted from her shoulders, and even though her bruised soul would take time to recover, she summoned an authentic smile.

She prayed ginger tea truly cured travel sickness, or it would be a very trying few months indeed.

"I shall not let you down, Mrs. Peagilly."

"I'm certain you shan't." Mrs. Peagilly fingered the pearls at her neck. "May I give you a piece of advice, Miss Roth?"

"Of course."

Should Faith remain in Lady Edyth's bedchamber or move her belongings to the servant's quarters attached to Mrs. Peagilly's room?

Common sense suggested the former would require far fewer explanations.

But could Faith listen to Lady Edyth's prattle and not betray herself?

"I would play your spat with Lord Constantine as a lover's tiff."

Lovers? Hardly. More like not quite enemies.

"Nothing more," Mrs. Peagilly continued. "Don't discuss it with anyone either. Not even Lady Charlotte or Lady Edyth."

Discuss what?

Faith stared at Mrs. Peagilly blankly for an instant.

Oh, the quarrel.

Seemingly unaware of Faith's wandering thoughts, Mrs. Peagilly pressed her fingertips together.

"Squabbles among betrothed are far more common than anyone admits. Even sweet Charlotte and my dear Wilfred have had a few spats, and he is a man of God. Nerves or cold feet and all of that, I suppose. I've never suffered from nerves, and my constitution has always been hardy."

She smiled, her eyes crinkling like fans at the corners.

"Mine as well." Faith had rarely even suffered a head cold as a child.

"Nevertheless," Mrs. Peagilly said, "until we depart Dovetonwick, I shall endeavor to be at your side whenever possible."

That afforded Faith much relief.

Otherwise, she'd either have to remain in her chamber, claiming an ailment that restricted her to her bed but didn't require a physician, or become a quick study at acting like an infatuated featherbrain. Neither was a palatable choice.

"Leave the Kellinggraves to explain to all and sundry why the betrothal was called off after you've gone." Mrs. Peagilly gave a sage nod and an arch look. "They can deal with the tattle, for in short order, we shall be on a ship bound for tropical climes to have the time of our lives."

"That sounds perfectly reasonable, Mrs. Peagilly."

And if not perfectly wonderful, at least far better than being unemployed, alone, and in London without sufficient funds to last more than a few months.

How long would it take for the scandalous dust to settle when she left with Mrs. Peagilly instead of Constantine?

As Faith was a nobody, not long, she'd venture.

Someone *le beau monde* deemed more important would

commit a faux pas, and the jackals would turn their sights onto another prey.

There was something to be said about being an inconsequential commoner.

The real question was, how long before Faith would *want* to return to England?

FOURTEEN

I shall be traveling outside of England soon and shall require a passport. As you've traveled extensively, I need your advice. How were you able to acquire a passport without knowledge of where you were born or providing information regarding your parentage?

Are there other traveling papers required for specific countries?

I am so looking forward to seeing you at Joy's...

~Miss Faith Roth, in a letter
to Miss Trinity Ablethorne,
started but not finished because
Lady Edyth entered the room

Dovetonwick Court stables
Two hours later

Faith hadn't left.

At least not by coach or horse. That knowledge should have brought Constantine a degree of peace, but it did not. His stomach remained a knotted ball of guilt and concern.

Everything within him told him she would find a way to flee. Not because she feared what the tattlemongers said, or that the fake betrothal was likely exposed, or because Constantine had disparaged her to Leopold.

No, Miss Faith Roth was too stalwart and intrepid to let those things deter her.

She'd leave because she couldn't face Constantine after his brutality.

Dual whips of remorse and regret upbraided him. It didn't matter that he hadn't known Faith hid behind the draperies and would never have opened his mouth had he been aware.

He closed his eyes for a blink.

Please, God. Give me a chance to make amends.

Constantine wasn't in the habit of praying, but if the good Lord saw fit to grant his petition and help repair the damage Constantine had inflicted, he'd start praying regularly. In fact, he'd make church attendance, Bible reading, and prayer part of his regime.

For a man of science and logic, true concessions, indeed.

What was that scripture his mother used to quote when he and his siblings squabbled, saying hurtful things and then claiming they didn't mean what they'd said in anger?

The things that come from a person's mouth come from the heart.

That truth scraped his conscience raw until he felt bloodied and bruised.

It was no more than he deserved.

He'd succumbed to his blasted pride and jealousy, causing Faith, the bravest, smartest, cleverest woman he knew, untold pain.

Hands on his hips, Constantine perused the tidy stable. Horses whickered and snorted equestrian greetings. The typical aromas of hay, horseflesh, and leather lingered in the air. Normally, nostalgia filled him when in the stables, bringing memories of hide-and-seek in the lofts or litters of sweet-faced mewling kittens and puppies. And newborn foals.

Not tonight.

No, tonight, self-recrimination blotted out happier times.

"And you're certain, Magnus, that no one has requested a conveyance or a horse saddled within the past two or three hours?" Constantine asked for the third—or was it the fourth?—time.

"Positive, Lord Constantine." Peering around the stalls, Magnus shook his head, nearly bald except for a fringe of pewter-gray hair curling over his large ears. "I've been here all evenin'. All the horses are accounted for, even the guests'. No one went anywhere unless they were on foot."

Faith wouldn't be that foolhardy.

It was four miles to Bishop's Knoll. Even with the moonlight, the trek to the small village was dark and foreboding, though there was little chance of wild animals attacking her. Besides, Edyth had checked her bedchamber an hour and a half ago on his behalf, and Faith hadn't removed her possessions.

She must be on Dovetonwick Court grounds, but where?

Having been discreetly apprised of the argument by Constantine, all the Kellinggraves covertly looked for Faith. No one asked what had transpired, but that didn't prevent his family from exchanging questioning glances.

Constantine puffed out a lungful of air.

Where the blazes was Faith, then?

It wasn't like her to sulk or hide, although he'd certainly given her reason to avoid him.

He'd done that in London too, though he'd used a different, unsuccessful tact. Shouldn't he be relieved and rejoicing that she'd given her notice?

Leopold hadn't said a word of reproach, but the censure in the cool gaze he gave Constantine when he'd informed their mother of the quarrel seared him with shame.

Honestly, Constantine didn't know what he could say to make recompense. He'd spoken a partial truth. Faith *had* been a pain in his bum and a source of frustration.

She wasn't any longer—at least not in the same manner.

Regardless, Faith Roth could aggravate the very devil with her sharp wit and eviscerating reposits, but what had once provoked Constantine's ire, he now considered one of her strengths. Confidence and self-assurance were something to be admired.

Faith could not leave Dovetonwick Court without talking to him. He wouldn't permit it, no matter her reluctance to see him. Constantine had made a grievous error, and he must apologize and somehow make it right.

How, he had no idea.

"No luck?" Leopold strolled in, his slightly rumpled jacket unbuttoned and a finger's worth of amber liquid in the glass he held. What the devil had he been doing to be in such a sorry state? He also perused the stables with his keen gaze. "Cedric's arrived. Thought you'd want to know."

Probably laughing himself to next Sunday at Constantine's predicament. For surely someone in the family had decided the middle Kellinggrave brother must be made aware of the fiasco.

Though they both lived in London, Constantine didn't see Cedric often. When he called upon his brother, most of the time, he was told Lieutenant Lord Cedric Kellinggrave was away from London on official business.

On a covert assignment, Constantine would wager.

"Oh, and Camberg-Trainer is looking for you," Leopold added before finishing the contents of his tumbler. "The fellow is in quite a dither."

Constantine's heart quickened.

Mayhap Harvey knew Faith's whereabouts.

"Let me know if you see anything, Magnus." Constantine rubbed his nose, suddenly bone weary. "Ask the other chaps to be alert too."

He doubted Faith would try to abscond with a horse, but desperate times and all of that rot.

Magnus scratched behind his ear. "Aye, sir."

As Constantine strode toward the house, Leopold ambled beside him. "You're certainly in a sorry state for someone who only a short while ago professed his adamant desire to be rid of a certain *mulish, opinionated termagant.*"

Constantine stopped mid-stride and pivoted to face his brother. "I know you find this highly amusing. I, however, do not. I hurt Faith, and that was never my intention. In point of fact, I respect her."

"Yes, that was abundantly clear." With a cocky grin, Leopold held up his glass in a mock salute. "I'd seek my mattress, but I cannot in good conscience embrace slumber with your Miss Roth missing. Deuced honor and all of that rot."

"I must find her, Leo."

Leopold threw an arm around Constantine's shoulder. "We shall, old chap. We shall."

They avoided the terrace, taking the route they had earlier in the evening, coming upon a couple partially hidden by shrubberies and the terrace wall in an intimate embrace.

Leopold elbowed Constantine and spoke low. "Is that our licentious cousin?"

Constantine squinted at the groping couple, who were still unaware they were being observed. "Indeed, and I believe that is Miss Breadalbane he's pawing. The chit cannot be more than seventeen."

"Martin has never been reluctant about despoiling innocents." Disgust weighted Leopold's tenor. "One of these days, he'll find himself on the field of honor."

"Ahem." Constantine cleared his throat loudly.

Martin and Miss Breadalbane sprang apart guiltily. Giggling, the chit covered her mouth before fluttering her fingers in a farewell wave then dashed away. Martin glowered, searching for Constantine concealed in the shadows, then sauntered off.

Constantine and Leopold continued on their way and entered the study, just as they had what seemed a lifetime ago. Constantine stopped so abruptly that Leopold plowed into his back.

Faith.

FIFTEEN

Such has been the chaos at Dovetonwick since I arrived that I haven't had an opportunity to continue my work. It's not likely I'll have the time either and shall have to postpone my plans until I return to London.

I've embroiled myself in a conundrum, the likes of which I could not have imagined. I am "betrothed" to Miss Faith Roth, my amanuensis, for the house party's duration. Instead of conducting valuable research, I must act the gallant while posturing and pretending to be smitten.

Oddly, because I find parties tedious and as pleasant as carbuncles on my arse, I do not mind Faith's company. In truth, I rather enjoy it. I never know what to expect from her, and I should detest that inconsistency. That I do not is wholly unnerving.

~Lord Constantine Kellinggrave,
jotting in his private journal

Dovetonwick Court's study
Three or four harrowing seconds later

There she sat composed and serene—*and beautiful*—looking for all the world like nothing had transpired to cut her to the quick.

Relief like he'd never known billowed over Constantine.

"I say," Leopold grumbled, but when he peeked over Constantine's shoulder, he said, "Oh, I see."

Faith sat demurely before Father's desk, Mrs. Peagilly in the chair beside her. A bemused Cedric lounged against the fireplace mantel, and with one hand on Father's shoulder, Mother stood beside him, seated behind his ridiculously large desk.

Charlotte and Edyth looked on, concern and apprehension puzzling their foreheads.

Of Wilfred Howerton, there was no sign.

"I see our lost dove has returned to the flock." Leopold had imbibed too freely. He started toward the liquor cabinet, but Father plucked the tumbler from his fingers.

"I think not, Leo."

Cedric chuckled and folded his arm. "If I'd known how entertaining this visit would be, I'd have made certain to arrive earlier."

"Cedric," the duchess admonished with regal firmness. "This is not a humorous matter."

"Actually, Mother, it is hilarious." Leopold planted his bum on the arm of the couch. "Not for Miss Roth, of course. She's an innocent victim."

Concern radiated from the apologetic gaze he momentarily turned upon Faith before jollity lit the depths of his gaze as he regarded Constantine.

Constantine flared his eyebrows.

Cedric flicked his fingers toward him. "But to see our pragmatic, brooding brother squirming... I'd pay for the opportunity."

"I am *not* brooding," Constantine said.

He wasn't.

Why did everyone mistake reserve for being taciturn or aloof?

Leopold waggled his eyebrows. "A leopard cannot change its spots, dear brother."

"Or a zebra it's stripes," Cedric put in sagely.

Idiots.

"Hush, you two." Charlotte's smile softened the rebuke.

"Did you know that zebras are actually black with white stripes?" Edyth announced, which caused everyone to stare at her. "Well, they are."

Folding her arms, she gave an exasperated huff and fell into sullen silence.

"I've seen many zebras, and you are correct, Lady Edyth."

Mrs. Peagilly's affirmation seemed to soothe Edyth's ruffled feathers.

"Faith...?" Constantine said before taking in his family's avid attention as one and all trained their inquisitive focus on him.

This was not a conversation he wanted to have with witnesses peering on. Instead, he sought to send them on their way. "Won't the guests become suspicious with all of us closeted in the study?"

Mother pursed her mouth and made a flippant wave of her hand.

"La. It's too late for that now. Ramona and Tabitha heard your quarrel with Miss Roth."

Devil a bit, they had.

Mother arched a perfectly plucked, disapproving eyebrow.

"They wasted no time informing me and, even now, are probably scurrying from guest to guest sharing the greatly embellished and exaggerated news."

"Gads," Edyth said. "Before it's all done, they will probably have Miss Roth slapping you for indecent advances."

The merest hint of pink tinged Faith's cheeks. Hopefully, the Kellinggraves would attribute the attractive coloring to bashfulness and not hit upon the truth. He and Faith had kissed.

And she had not slapped him. No, indeed.

Only by biting the inside of his cheek did Constantine curb the primal male smile that tried to bend his mouth upward. He probably looked like he'd swallowed something foul, but better that than his far too astute family stumbling upon the truth.

"It's not as serious as all that," Father said, sitting back in his chair and folding his hands over his slight paunch. "Everyone knows those two prattle brains haven't the acumen of a sparrow, and anyone with any sense disregards most of what they say."

Harsh words from Father, who seldom remarked darkly upon anyone's character.

"Ahem." Faith cleared her throat, drawing everyone's attention back to her once more. "As I was saying, before Lord Constantine and Lord Kenworthy arrived, I have accepted a position as companion to Mrs. Peagilly. We sail for the Mediterranean next month."

No! You cannot leave.

For a horrifying moment, Constantine feared he'd shouted aloud. It took several more heartbeats for his breathing to resume after the bludgeoning to his soul that Faith's revelation caused.

Who will transcribe my notes?

If possible, he'd kick himself in the arse for his despicable shallowness.

Notes, you dimwitted dolt?

Faith's worth went far beyond her scrivener duties.

"That is wonderful," Charlotte said with a wide smile. "If I weren't getting married, I would envy you."

"I certainly do." Edyth shrugged when several astonished gazes swung at her. "I've always wanted to go on a grand adventure, but no one ever asks me what *I* want."

"You are too fond of bathing, wearing clean clothing, and sleeping on a soft mattress, Edie," Cedric jested. "Trust me, dear sister. The reality of grand adventures is not glamorous or romantic."

His tone took on a harshness around the edges.

Yes, definitely an agent of the crown.

Edyth stuck her tongue out at him and gave Cedric an exaggerated pout. "You're home less than an hour and already a teasing beast."

"Hush, children," Mother admonished. "Miss Roth was speaking."

"Thank you, Your Grace." Speaking with the aplomb of an Almack's peeress, Faith straightened her shoulders a fraction. "I shall continue with the betrothal charade until after the wedding, and to curtail gossip, I shall stay in Lady Edyth's bedchamber, if that's acceptable."

"Of course it is, dear Faith!" Edyth's enthusiasm caused Father to spare her an indulgent smile. "I've planned hot chocolate and shortbread for us tonight."

"That is most kind of you, Lady Edyth." Faith's eyes softened with sincere affection before she addressed the duchess again. "That is if you can assure me that Mercy and Ronan Brockman are not guests. I thought I saw Mercy earlier, and if she is here, she will know that I am not affianced."

Charlotte and Mother exchanged puzzled glances.

"Never fear, Miss Roth," the duchess said. "Naturally, we are acquainted with the Brockmans, but 'tis Constantine who boasts a close friendship with Brockman. They are not amongst those invited to the house party and wedding."

Faith tilted her head. "Very well. I do insist on minimal contact with Lord Constantine."

Constantine hid a wince.

She might as well have landed him a facer.

One of Constantine's brothers choked back a laugh, but he didn't spare them a glance to see which. Let them have their fun at his expense. Their day would come, and he'd be the one chortling at their discomfit.

Faith continued as if she hadn't heard the rude noise and spoke directly to the duke and duchess. "That should pave the way for you to announce that the betrothal's been broken when I leave with Mrs. Peagilly in three days."

The whole while she spoke in that sultry contralto, she avoided meeting Constantine's eyes.

How, by thunder, had she and Mrs. Peagilly put their heads together and devised this scheme in the space of two hours?

Faith couldn't go off exploring God only knew where with the elderly woman.

"Are you certain that's a good idea?" Constantine advanced a couple of feet, willing Faith to meet his eyes. "Two women cavorting around the world? All manner of appalling things might happen to you."

Faith raised her head, her gaze clashing with his, and that stubborn chin took on the angle he'd come to recognize as defiance. Gone were her soft brown doe eyes. In their place were flinty, obsidian orbs.

"Appalling things can happen anywhere, Lord Constantine."

"Touché, Miss Roth." Leopold accompanied his glib reply with two fingers to his forehead in a respectful salute.

Her bowed mouth curved slightly, and Leopold's face split into a broad grin.

Fiend seize it. Leo was truly taken with her.

She returned her attention to Constantine. "As I am *not* your wife, betrothed, employee, servant, or slave, what I do is none of your concern."

She enunciated the last four words in a clipped staccato.

Cedric exchanged a hilarity-filled glance with Leopold, and they smothered another round of chuckles with pathetically false coughs.

Brothers.

It took all of Constantine's restraint not to gnash his teeth. Instead, he sent a glance heavenward.

A little help here, please?

"If I may..." Mrs. Peagilly lifted her hand, and after offering everyone a benevolent closed-mouth smile said, "I've been traveling the world for longer than you've been alive, Lord Constantine. I assure you, I am well acquainted with possible mishaps, and I take every measure to prevent them."

A positively precocious glint entered her eyes. "I'll admit to a moment of disconcertment when I found a python curled upon my cot, but I had left the tent unfastened, so I could not blame the poor creature."

Mother gasped and clasped her throat as Edyth grasped Charlotte's hands, and they both turned pale as chalk.

Cedric's and Leopold's jaws sagged to their chests, but Father laughed.

No. Absolutely not.

Faith was not going anywhere where snakes capable of

consuming humans slithered into tents and took a comfy lie down on a cot.

No, by God above, not as long as the sun rose and set. As long as robins sang and butterflies pollinated.

"On your cot, you say?" Rubbing his chin, Father gave a bemused shake of his head. "Asleep?"

"Indeed. Content as a kitten." Mrs. Peagilly rose and waited for Faith to do the same. "It was only four feet long. A wee little thing, actually. I was in no real danger."

"*Four* feet?" Charlotte croaked.

"The largest I've seen was eighteen feet," Mrs. Peagilly said with the calmness of a woman speaking about a favorite dainty at tea or a knitting pattern.

"Oh, my word." Mother looked rather ill.

Mrs. Peagilly leveled her inscrutable gaze upon Constantine. "You may rest assured. Miss Roth's safety will not be compromised while in *my* company."

Was she implying Miss Roth had been compromised in other ways while in Constantine's company?

Just what had Faith told the perceptive old bird?

"As it's been a rather, ah, eventful evening, I'll bid you good night." Faith stood, displaying the innate grace he'd taken for granted these many weeks. Along with her voluptuous, plump lips, the porcelain slope of her cheeks, and melted chocolate eyes that made a man imagine all sorts of things he shouldn't.

"Faith, a word?" Constantine asked, softening what sounded more like a command with, "Please?"

He didn't give a tinker's oath if he sounded desperate or if his highly amused brothers grinned like pished baboons. Or that his mother considered him with an unnerving mélange of calculation, discernment, and astonishment.

Did Father conceal a ghost of a smile behind his hand?

There was nothing for it.

Constantine's gut told him that if he didn't seize the moment, Faith would be lost to him. His well-organized, predictable world was unraveling at an alarming rate, and he had no more ability to temper the chaos than a leaf slipping over a waterfall.

Her expression solemn and sad—so sad, it sliced Constantine to the marrow, and he felt the blood gushing from him—Faith skimmed her turbulent brown eyes, framed by trembling lashes, over his face.

What did she seek?

He'd far rather she bristled with indignation. Raised a breeze and called him a knave, a curt beast, an inconsiderate tosspot. Shred him with her rapier tongue.

She shook her head, forlornness having replaced her feisty spirit.

"No. Neither of us wishes to say anything further to wound the other. Sometimes the best course is silence. It's wiser and kinder."

And with that, she tucked her hand into the bend of Mrs. Peagilly's thin arm and escorted the dame from the drawing room.

Everything around Constantine faded into a haze.

His focus remained trained on Faith as she walked away. If he felt this desolate when she simply left the room, how would he survive when she walked out of his life in three days?

And there was nothing he could do to stop it.

Nothing.

SIXTEEN

It is astonishing how one's life can take a dramatic turn in one day, even an hour, or a few minutes. While at the Duke and Duchess of Landrith's house party to which I was compelled to attend by my employer, I've resigned my position as amanuensis to Lord Constantine Kellinggrave and have accepted a position as a traveling companion to Mrs. Eustasia Peagilly. I shall explain all when I see you at your soirée if opportunity and time allow. I'm reluctant to put the details to pen.

I sail for the Mediterranean in October and do not know when I shall return to England.

I have also decided to never wed—matrimony was never at the top of my list of things to accomplish in any event. Men are incorrigible, unscrupulous, self-centered beasts.

~Miss Faith Roth, in a letter accepting
Mrs. Joy Morrisette's invitation

Early the next morning

Having spent a sleepless night, first staring at the canopy above Lady Edyth's luxurious bed and then at the crack between the draperies for two hours before dawn's subtle hues crept over the horizon, Faith slipped her feet into her half-boots as she sat on a tufted gold bench in one of the upper corridors.

The early morning sounds of a house awakening filtered to her as she laced her boots, then donned the Pomona green spencer. Conversations between servants drifted into corridors as doors opened and closed, swift footsteps echoed along passageways, and cows lowed in the distance as a rooster exuberantly greeted the sunrise.

Normally an early riser, she didn't share his enthusiasm today.

Not with an ache niggling behind her left eye and a head that felt stuffed with wet wool from lack of sleep, stifling sighs so she wouldn't disturb Lady Edyth's slumber, and no small amount of fretting over her future too. And, if she were wholly honest—which she tried to be even if facing the truth was uncomfortable—a weird, undefinable grief and a penetrating sense of failure.

She'd arisen fifteen minutes ago and, with stealth that would've done a seasoned agent of the Crown justice, had washed, dressed in a plain jonquil day dress, wound her waist-length hair into a simple chignon, and tiptoed from the bedchamber with shoes, spencer, and hat in hand while Lady Edyth slept on.

All through the night, an urgency had been building inside Faith to escape the house.

Oh, not to flee like a vagrant caught stealing a silver candlestick, but to put distance between her and Constantine. Knowing he slept beneath the same roof was too...intimate.

Outside the mansion, she could breathe in the fresh morning air and sort her tumultuous thoughts. Her emotions had undergone so many ups and downs in the past four and twenty hours than if they had been a coach ride, she'd have cast up her accounts a dozen times.

As the grand ball was tonight, the rest of the day was certain to be an unbearable strain. The duchess had Nita remaking one of Lady Charlotte's gowns, and the final fitting was to be mid-morning. Last night, amid rapturous sighs and excited giggles, hot chocolate and shortbread, Lady Edyth had exclaimed that the entire afternoon would be spent preparing for the ball.

For heaven's sake.

An entire afternoon?

What could possibly take so blasted long?

Faith meant to keep her word, nevertheless. She'd attend the ball, perhaps even dance and pretend she was having a brilliant time. She intended to avoid Constantine the entire while, and when she could not evade him, she'd treat him with cool formality. Her resolve to put him out of her life might waver if she regarded him with anything other than icy disdain.

After descending two flights of stairs, she paused, swinging her bonnet by its saffron-colored ribbons.

Where was the kitchen?

Faith hoped to cajole the cook out of an apple, a scone, or a piece of bread and cheese to enjoy on her outing. She wasn't picky, but she was famished. She'd barely touched dinner, and Faith enjoyed her meals without apologizing for her robust appetite.

Lady Edyth said ladies generally ate nothing during the day in preparation for the magnificent midnight supper.

Midnight?

By all that was holy, Faith wasn't waiting until midnight to fill her belly.

A pretty maid bustled down the corridor. Head down and humming, she carried a stack of neatly folded towels. She released a little yelp when she glanced up and saw Faith.

"Forgive me, Miss. You startled me. Guests are rarely up this early."

"I'm sorry." Offering a repentant smile, Faith looped her bonnet over her arm. "I was looking for the kitchen. I want to take a walk and hoped I might convince the cook to permit me a little something for breakfast."

A grin crinkling her face, the maid adjusted her load and then tilted her head in the direction she'd come.

"Follow this corridor past the last door on the right, then turn right. You'll see a flight of stairs halfway down that passageway to your left. Take them, and they'll lead you directly to the kitchen."

"Thank you…"

"Alma." The girl pulled a face. "I was named after my grandmother."

"Thank you, Alma." Faith fished a coin from her pocket and handed it to the wide-eyed girl. "You've been most helpful."

Another pleased grin split Alma's freckled face. "If you need anything, miss, you just ask me."

She took a swift, furtive peek up and down the corridor before stepping closer.

"I never paid any of that tattle about you being Lord Constantine's mistress any mind, Miss. Anybody who knows him knows he's an honorable gentleman. I'm glad he's found someone so nice to marry."

Before Faith could respond, Alma resumed her humming and her trek to the upper story to deliver towels to guests.

Faith wasn't certain whether to be relieved or annoyed that even the servants had heard the ugly rumors. Although the truth was that servants always knew what went on in a house, even when the residents didn't.

A ghost of a smile played around the edges of her mouth as she followed Alma's directions to the kitchen. At least someone hadn't believed the tattle, even if it was only a maid.

The aromas of coffee, ham, and something sweet and spicy filtered to her as Faith descended the narrow stairway.

She inhaled deeply.

Heavenly.

Her stomach gurgled its appreciation too.

Hesitant and reluctant to intrude, she paused at the hospitable but immaculate kitchen's threshold.

"Good mornin' to ye, miss. May I be of assistance?"

A rotund, red-cheeked woman with a profusion of frizzy gray-blonde curls sticking out from beneath her mob cap wiped her hands on her crisp, no-nonsense apron as she trundled forward.

"Um, yes. I wondered if perhaps I might have an early breakfast? Just an apple or a piece of bread to take with me on a walk?"

"Pshaw, nothin' for it." The cook marched across the kitchen, pointing to a well-used corner table. "Have a seat, miss. I'll have ye fed in nae time."

Faith hadn't planned on lingering in the kitchen, but her stomach growled again. Loudly.

She pressed a hand to her middle.

Her eyes twinkling, Cook asked, "Do ye favor cinnamon buns?"

That was what the scrumptious smell was.

"I do."

Faith couldn't recall the last time she enjoyed such a scrumptious indulgence.

Mouth practically watering, she settled onto a hardback chair, observing the servants as they efficiently performed their tasks. Friendly teasing and good-natured rivalry punctuated their conversations. This was a well-run home with content, happy domestics.

That said much about the Landriths.

A bashful girl of no more than twelve brought Faith tea, milk, and sugar. She dipped an awkward curtsy. "Here you are, miss. I nipped the sugar this morning."

"Thank you very much." It was brown sugar, not the precious white sugar reserved for those above stairs. Faith didn't give a farthing.

Blushing, the girl, probably the scullery maid, scampered away.

"Start peelin' those potatoes n' carrots, Mary," the cook said as the girl passed. "And then scrub the beets."

"Yes, ma'am."

Too bad the child had to work as a domestic, and it was likely if she'd ever had any formal education, that phase of her life was over. And yet, Faith felt certain the child was grateful for her position. In a grand house such as this, she was assured to always be well-fed and have a warm bed.

As Faith poured the fragrant tea into a plain white teacup, no doubt the servant's crockery, she idly observed the staff and pondered the wisdom of dawdling for a few minutes to eat.

What were the chances someone else—namely Constantine—would pay a visit to the kitchen this early? Miniscule. Faith had left her chamber at ten after five and hadn't encountered another soul other than Alma.

Confident she could enjoy breakfast uninterrupted, she plopped two lumps of sugar into her tea and stirred. She nearly sighed aloud when Cook placed a plate laden with ham, coddled eggs, sausage, toast, and the promised sweet roll before her.

"Take all the time ye need, miss." Cook winked. "There's more if yer still hungry."

Examining the heaping plate, Faith laughed. "This will suffice."

The cook returned a moment later with butter, preserves, and a bowl of sliced strawberries.

"Thank you." Faith helped herself to two of the juicy red berries.

"Primrose Pumilia Pippenger, my sweet."

Faith whisked her attention to the doorway.

Who...?

SEVENTEEN

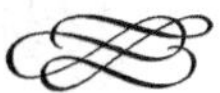

After your last refusal, I wouldn't ask you again if the situation wasn't dire. I've spoken to the debtors myself this time. Martin has until December first to pay them, or it's to debtors' prison for him. I haven't the blunt to cover his debts. Tabitha and Ramona have a constant stream of bills coming in. I know my son has faults, but what father can watch his child go to prison?

~Lord Hayward Kellinggrave, in a letter
to his brother Harland Kellinggrave,
Duke of Landrith

Still in Dovetonwick Court's kitchen
Three uncomfortable seconds later

A man's voice—*please not Constantine, please not Constantine*—far too high-spirited and jolly for this time of the morning accompanied the staccato of boot heels in the corridor.

A delighted grin wreathed the cook's face as she hurried back to the stove to turn over the ham.

"Do I smell cinnamon buns?" the man asked as he drew closer to the kitchen. "*Please* tell me I smell cinnamon buns."

Having just filled her mouth with an ample bite of ham and toast, Faith almost choked. Eyes watering, she swallowed twice and then took a gulp of hot tea, burning her tongue.

Drat and damna—

Faith stopped herself just short of cursing aloud.

She might've become a liar via coercion, but she wasn't going to start muttering vulgarities beneath her breath.

Another forceful swallow propelled the lodged food down her throat. The alternative was spewing a mouthful of half-chewed ham and toast across the table.

Not precisely ladylike.

But then again, Faith wasn't a lady, per se, was she?

Not by birth, but she'd been raised with the skills and decorum of the noblest aristocrat.

Of course, the man approaching wasn't Constantine, she reassured herself.

What was she thinking?

He was never cheerful, light-hearted, or playful.

Besides, Faith knew his rumbling voice well.

Dry, critical, acerbic... and any number of appropriate and unflattering descriptions for a man with no sense of humor, who often forgot to comb his hair, and preferred insects to people.

Most likely, the overly chipper chap was one of his older brothers.

Still, Faith must be gone from the kitchen before whoever he was entered. She wasn't in the mood for conversation or explanations, and she felt certain Lord Cedric or Lord Kenworthy would expect one or both.

Faith slapped her bonnet on her head, letting the ribbons dangle. She grabbed the toast, sausage, and sweet bun and, after plopping them in the middle of the napkin, vaulted to her feet.

Dovetonwick's laundress would never forgive her for the offense to the linen square.

Once Faith had snatched the corners together, she rushed to the door on the other side of the kitchen, praying whoever the exuberant fellow was, she'd make her escape before he entered.

Aware of several perplexed or amused gazes fixed upon her, she raised a forefinger to her lips. "Shh. I was never here."

A lad of perhaps seventeen years broke into a cheeky grin, two fresh-faced maids covered their mouths and giggled, and Cook puffed her cheeks out as if stifling what she yearned to say.

Faith slipped through the doorway, confident she'd made her getaway undetected by whichever Kellinggrave male believed—as she did—that mornings were the prime time of day.

"Why, Miss Roth. Are you breaking your fast without me? I thought we agreed on half-past five?"

Oh, bugger.

There was no need for Faith to look to know that every person in the room stared at her as she stood, frozen, one foot in the air like a deranged flamingo. Her chest deflated on a sigh as she reluctantly lowered her foot and, clutching the small bundle of food to her waist, slowly pivoted.

"I do not recall any such arrangement, my lord."

Because there wasn't one.

Regardless, Faith couldn't very well call Constantine a liar in front of the help. It just wasn't done.

"No harm done." Lord Constantine bowed with the

ridiculous flourish of a court courier. "If you're so anxious to depart, I shall bring my breakfast too."

Faith rolled her eyes ceilingward. Served her right for coveting the cinnamon bun.

He turned to the beaming cook and flashed a disarming smile. "Cook dearest, put a piece of ham between two slices of bread, will you? I'll also take two cinnamon buns."

"Of course, yer lordship." A wide smile divided Cook's face as she bustled to do his bidding.

Lord Constantine clearly had the woman wrapped around his little finger. Faith had never seen this side of him. Charming and carefree and...and by George, playful.

Lord Constantine Kellinggrave was playful.

More than one female servant eyed him approvingly from beneath her lashes, and a queer unpleasant sensation rooted around Faith's stomach at their obvious interest.

Not jealousy.

Nothing could be farther from the truth or more absurd.

Ridiculous.

What had he called the cook?

Primrose Pumilia Pippenger.

Surely not the woman's real name. If so, someone had done the poor dear a disservice.

Faith cast a longing glance out the door, absently noting the tidy kitchen garden with its carefully tended rows of herbs and vegetables. She shifted her gaze over the dry rock wall bordering one side of the garden to the pasture beyond.

If she hadn't been so greedy, she might be trudging across yonder meadow even now, munching on the cinnamon bun.

His strides long and sleek, Constantine sauntered over, and though he wore his usual self-assured smile, sympathy and kindness warmed his green eyes.

Bolster yourself. Raise your ramparts.

That Faith had to tell herself to be on guard didn't bode well.

Cognizant of the ears cocked and trying to hear their every word, Faith whispered. "Lord Constantine, I don't desire company."

He continued to smile indulgently at her.

"I'm simply going for a walk in the meadows." Really, must he keep smiling at her in that rakish fashion? And, confound it, must her silly pulse quicken because he did?

His smile broadened incrementally as if he knew precisely what she was about and meant to thwart her plans regardless.

Fine. Two could play that game.

Fashioning an innocent smile, she angled her head to meet his amused gaze. Why must he be so dashed tall? It was rather discomposing to take someone down a peg while craning one's neck.

"I plan to spend time in deep prayer and seek the Lord's guidance, not conversation," she said.

There. That ought to put Constantine off. Any moment, he'd pivot and dart out the door.

"Nevertheless, I shall accompany you," he whispered back

What? She drew back and blinked up at him. *No.*

He is supposed to let me go alone.

Then Constantine winked as if he'd read her riotous thoughts.

The bounder winked as if he hadn't shredded her heart with his cold arrogance yesterday.

Well, Faith wasn't falling for that rogue's ploy.

For as it says in *The Court and Character of King James* by Anthony Weldon:

He that deceives me once, it's his fault; but if twice, it's my fault.

She wasn't about to be taken in by a handsome face,

mesmerizing green eyes, or a disarming smile again. Don't forget his hewn jaw and muscular shoulders and chest.

Stop it!

Faith steadfastly focused on Constantine's shiny boots until her traitorous gaze began to climb his sleek, sculpted legs. *No!*

What the devil was wrong with her?

He called you a mulish, opinionated termagant.

Clenching her jaw in irritation, Faith swiftly switched her attention to the small bundle clutched to her middle. She would not meet Constantine's eyes because if she did, she might—very likely, in truth—forget her resolve to treat him like a stranger.

Cook brought him a basket covered with a blue and white linen cloth.

"Yer lordship. I also packed enough for Miss Roth since ye interrupted her breakfast."

"Thank you, Pip." He dropped a peck onto her plump cheek, and Cook's already flushed cheeks turned a brighter shade of red.

"Go on with ye, young rascal." She pointed her gaze at Faith. "Mind yer manners with yer betrothed."

"I always do," he quipped.

Faith shot him a reproving look but swallowed her building rancor when she saw the rakish tilt of his lips.

He was jesting.

Who was this man?

Where had the brusque beast who couldn't abide her presence gone to?

She'd expect this behavior from his brothers, for from what she'd seen, they were the flippant gallants. The rapscallions and rogues of the family. Not Constantine. He was the serious brother.

Once outside, Constantine plucked her mashed napkin from her fingers and dropped the blob into the basket. "You've squished whatever is in that napkin to a pulp. I daresay it's unfit to eat."

He was right, but his highhandedness still vexed her.

Pulling her eyebrows together and pinching her lips tight, Faith drew in a calming breath. She would not lose her temper. "I suppose there is nothing I can say that will dissuade you from accompanying me."

"Not a thing," he affirmed with a cheeky grin.

Of course, there wasn't.

Faith had known he'd say that before she asked, but nevertheless, she'd hoped...

She turned toward the pathway leading to the side of the house.

Gilly spied her and bounded to her side, offering a doggy grin.

Scratching behind his scruffy ears, she considered bolting.

Would Constantine pursue her if she hoisted her skirts and pelted off like a recalcitrant child?

Probably.

He wore no hat or gloves, and upon closer inspection, it looked as if a toddler had tied his rumpled neckcloth. As usual, it appeared he'd combed his hair with his fingers. The unruly, slightly messy style suited him.

Had he dressed in a rush?

Why?

She kicked at a pebble, taking her frustration out on the rock. "Why?"

Bother and blast, she'd said that aloud.

He didn't know what she'd been thinking. He'd assume she referred to his earlier statement.

Gilly darted off to explore the long grass, barking every now and then at a canine discovery.

The seconds ticked onward as Faith walked several paces, and still he didn't answer. At last, she gave him a side-eyed glance. Surprised to see him regarding her with such warmth and affection, she stumbled.

At once, his strong hand encircled her elbow and steadied her.

"Let's just say I'm not ready to quit the field just yet." He released her arm and pointed his attention forward.

Faith gaped at him.

Ready to quit...

What?

She needed to set him straight at once.

"My lord, if you are under the misconception that I shall change my mind, you are wrong."

It would be the height of folly to do so. Faith would have to be out of her bloody, everlasting mind. And *that* she assuredly was not. There was something to be said for self-preservation and all of that fribble.

"After the things you said..." She bit her tongue. Repeating those caustic words would benefit no one.

"I spoke out of anger and frustration, Faith, but that's no excuse. My behavior was unforgivable."

With a heart-wrenchingly gentle smile, Constantine stopped and tipped her chin upward with his free hand. He dropped a kiss on her nose, and after the little quivers of desire stopped assailing her, Faith's heart tumbled to lay at his booted feet. Any more of that flirtation or seduction or whatever it was, and she feared her heart would be his to do with as he wished.

Blast the man.

This is exactly what she didn't want to happen.

"We need to talk, Faith."

"We are talking right now."

An enigmatic smile tipped Constantine's much too shapely mouth up rakishly on one side, and he grazed his bent knuckle over her jaw.

Faith's mind stalled, and her pulse capered along her veins like a frisky lamb.

"You are the most confounding yet captivating woman."

For reasons she'd never understand, his lowly murmured words in that resonating baritone pleased her greatly, though she wasn't positive they were meant as a compliment.

"Fine. Say what you will, my lord, and let's be done with it then."

She made certain to address him formally to keep distance between them.

Giving him another sideways look, she shook her head, then jiggled her finger at him for good measure.

He really must take her seriously.

"But know that you shan't change my mind. I shall leave with Mrs. Peagilly and sail to the Mediterranean in October. I am set on it. My course cannot be changed."

Even if it meant breaking her heart, for Faith had come to realize that Lord Constantine Kellinggrave was not a man a woman could be around day after day and remain immune to him. He was also not a man a woman could walk away from and not leave a part of her soul behind.

Faith's intent was to leave as little as possible of her heart in his keeping when they permanently parted ways.

Too late.

Stupid, stupid, foolish girl for not guarding herself against the feelings that had been growing for weeks. When he'd been gruff, obtuse, and annoying, it had been easy to dismiss the sentiment unfurling in her heart.

But when he'd been kind and considerate, funny and playful... Well, her traitorous heart had unlocked and opened wide.

Now she was in a fine pickle, indeed.

"I can be very persuasive," he all but purred.

Yes, that was precisely what Faith was afraid of.

Constantine winked again before beginning to whistle, quite exceptionally, in fact.

He whistled too?

What else didn't she know about this man?

She'd wager as much as he didn't know about her. And because their relationship ended in just a couple of short days, she wasn't trying to find out anything more about him. She'd bear the scars of their acquaintance for the rest of her days as it was.

Instead, she touched his arm and, to divert him, asked, "Constantine, is Cook's name really Primrose Pumilia Pippenger?"

EIGHTEEN

*As Mr. Petheringham's last letter contains what I
perceive to be a threat, I cannot help but speculate that
perhaps he is, in fact, John Smith; the man who brought the
child to Haven House and Academy for the Enrichment of
Young Women. I also cannot help but wonder if his obsession with finding Bernadette Rennison—known as Faith
Roth now—after all these years is not merely familial
concern but perhaps something more nefarious.*

*Toward that end, I wish to retain your services and ask
that you continue the investigation your predecessor began.
I shall be in London next week and should like to meet with
you then. Miss Roth and I are attending a soirée in a
couple of weeks, and I hope to be able to reassure her that she
has nothing to fear. I have warned her of Mr.
Petheringham's persistence and asked her not to agree to see
him until we know exactly who he is and his motives.*

*I have enclosed a deposit and shall pay the balance
when we meet.*

~Mrs. Hester Shepherd, in a short letter

to Detective Cyril Dankworth

Dovetonwick Court
Kitchen garden pathway
A minute later

Constantine burst into laughter.

Would Faith never cease to surprise him?

Expression grave, she appeared so earnest, so intent, that he'd expected a far more personal question.

Why are you such a cad to me?

Why have you treated me with such undeserved contempt?

Why did you lie about meeting me for breakfast?

When he'd wrestled his mirth under control, he nodded. "Indeed. Her parents christened her Primrose Pumilia, and she married a sailor named Rafferty Pippinger."

"Oh." Faith's rosy lips twitched, her eyes sparkling with suppressed mirth. "It's quite a mouthful, isn't it?"

"Most everyone addresses her as Pip." He switched the heavy basket to his other arm.

What had Pip packed?

A banquet for six?

Adjusting the basket so it hung over his bent arm, he scanned the cart path they strolled along. "Edyth alerted me that you'd crept out of her chamber before the cock crowed."

"I could've sworn she was asleep." Faith flattened her mouth into a thin line. Edyth's loyalty to Constantine peeved her. "I was so careful not to wake her."

"She was worried about you," Constantine offered by way of an explanation. "She likes you very much."

Well, that made one Kellinggrave who did.

Faith shrugged as she turned off the track and onto the lush grass toward a fence. "She needn't have been. I've been taking care of myself for a long time. I walk to your laboratory every morning at six o'clock. London's streets are far more dangerous than an early morning meander through a field. It's not likely a cow will rob me."

Constantine flared his nose on a sharp intake of air. "You *walk* to work every day?"

It took her over an hour. Every day. On London's streets? *Good Lord*.

Did she know how dangerous that was?

Faith gave him an incredulous look as she lifted her skirts and nimbly clambered up the fence rail.

He tried, unsuccessfully, to ignore her well-turned ankle and shapely calves.

What other woman of his acquaintance would've clambered over the fence without assistance? Edyth might've done; if no one was around to see her. But he couldn't conceive of another female he knew even attempting the feat.

Straddled over the top rail, Faith shoved a burnished blonde curl brushing her cheek behind her ear.

"How did you think I made my way there, my lord?"

"I...ah..." In point of fact, Constantine hadn't once considered it.

Chagrin chafed his conscience. He was the worst sort of inconsiderate blackguard.

"Not all of us have coaches and carriages, gigs and curricles, or horses at our disposal, my lord."

Or the funds to hire a hackney to and from work every day.

After hopping to the ground, she held her hand out, and he stared at it blankly. "The basket, if you please?"

"Oh. Yes." He jiggled it up and down. "It's quite heavy. Pip always packs too much food."

"I think I can manage," Faith said dryly.

He passed it to her and then, laying one hand atop the top rail, vaulted over the fence. As he collected the basket once more, he pointed to a gnarled oak tree atop a knoll.

The upper branches had been one of his favorite places to hide as a child when he wanted time alone. He'd intruded on Faith's time alone, but only because he wanted to talk with her in private and without interruptions.

Neither were likely to occur inside the mansion.

"We can eat there, Faith. It's a bit of a hike, but the view is splendid. It overlooks Tiplewater Beck on the far side, sheep and cattle on the other, and you can see Bishop's Knoll in the distance."

"What about Gilly?" Putting a hand to her forehead to shield her eyes, she searched the adjacent fields.

"He'll find his way home." He always did. Gilly would explore for a bit before he'd return to the house or stables.

Faith made a sound between a grunt and a snort as she stomped up the incline.

No one would ever call her a proper lady.

Thank God.

What did Constantine want with a proper lady anyway?

He trailed behind, trying to sort out his thoughts and determine what he would say. The gentle sway of Faith's trim hips as she ascended the hillock with ease mesmerized him.

A jay's harsh call echoed from the woodlands bordering the far meadows. Another jay answered with an equally raucous reply.

Wildlife abounded in the woodlands and meadows.

This is where Constantine first fell in love with nature as a tyke, and with butterflies and moths later. Ironically, he wasn't too keen on their larva, but that was a carefully guarded secret. Worms, grubs, larvae, caterpillars...anything long that crawled, especially snakes, gave him the shivers.

Halfway up the hillside, Faith paused. Hands on her hips, she swept her gaze across the area. Low on the horizon, the sun peeked forth in its glorious splendor like a shy debutante at her first ball.

Would Faith be bashful and nervous tonight?

He felt certain she'd never attended anything as grand and majestic as a ball hosted by the Duke and Duchess of Landrith.

No, he'd be right there at her side the entire time to assure Faith was not overwhelmed. Although, he doubted much dazed Faith Roth. She was the most intrepid, self-assured, and fearless woman he'd ever known who hadn't been born into privilege, wealth, and station.

"I forgot how much I like the country," she said. "I haven't been outside London since leaving the academy where I was raised and educated."

Constantine came alongside her. "A home and school for orphans?"

"Not exactly." She scrunched her nose. "Haven House and Academy for the Enrichment of Young Women is where the toplofty dispose of unwanted female progeny. Illegitimate, orphaned, abandoned, inconvenient, the product of affairs, by-blows... It's not cheap, but confidentiality and discretion are assured."

"Do you know where you came from? Who your family is?" he asked, not wanting to pry but genuinely interested in knowing more about her.

He stepped over a large stone, startling a brown hairstreak butterfly sunning itself.

"No. None of us do, although a few girls have been able to uncover the truth once they leave the academy."

She pushed her bonnet off her head and let it dangle down her back. As was her wont, she wore no gloves. She possessed slim fingers with well-tended, oval-shaped nails, and somehow, she'd managed to rid the pink flesh of ink stains.

His own digits still bore a smudge or two, and he'd scrubbed them with pumice.

"We do know we were unwanted. Our names were changed to protect the identity of whoever decided we were inconvenient. Mrs. Shepherd, the proprietress, gave each of us a biblical name, and we all carry a version of her surname as well, Shepherd. She says we are all her daughters."

"And do you know your given name?"

They were nearly to the top. Constantine's breath came quicker as the incline steepened.

A pair of turtle doves took to wing at his approach. Probably nesting in the oak. They preferred dense pines, but as they built up to six nests each season, a pair wasn't always particular where they constructed a nest.

The sun had edged higher in the sky, feathering the drowsy sky in hues of amber, lavender, and peach. Early mornings were Constantine's favorite time of day. It was a rare day indeed that he stayed abed past five.

"No." She shook her head, causing that loose tendril to spring loose again. "We aren't told anything about our origins on purpose."

A nuance of regret whisked across Faith's porcelain features.

She cared more than she let on.

"They're carefully guarded secrets. It's all part of the agreement. Girls are provided a home, an education, and training for a profession. We are never meant to know anything about our families."

She fingered the yellow-green ribbon tied at her neck.

"When I consider the alternatives, I'm grateful. At least someone cared enough to ensure I was provided for. I wasn't abandoned on the street. That's something, isn't it?"

Those mesmerizing eyes searched Constantine's, a tinge of uncertainty in hers.

Growing up knowing you were unwanted—an inconvenience—even if the academy was a remarkably unique institution must've been heartbreaking.

He made an affirmative sound in his throat. "It's more than many have, but knowing you as I do, you'd rather know the truth. Sordid, scandalous, and all."

She chuckled and pulled her bonnet back on.

"Sometimes I think I want to know, and other times..." She lifted her shoulders. "I don't really care."

They'd reached the top. Slightly out of breath, Faith asked, "What difference would it make? It's not as if I'd track down my family and show up at their doorstep. They didn't want me."

No bitterness or rancor laced her voice.

Unlike Martin, she'd accepted her lot in life.

Constantine's heart twinged for her, nonetheless.

He'd grown up surrounded by a loving family who, even when perturbed with him, would all rally to his side if he needed them.

They would rally to Faith's too. If she were your wife.

Hold there, he chastised his conscience.

Yes, Constantine wanted Faith to stay on as his scrivener, but he wasn't in love with her. Not once had he gone mooneyed, awkward, and tongue-tied as his friends and Harvey were wont to do, though each would deny it. Their masculine pride wouldn't allow for the vulnerability being in love created.

True, Faith had caused Constantine a sleepless night or two or ten, and he'd spent a good deal of time thinking about her. But in London, it was because she exasperated him to no end, and here, he'd been concerned about the uncomfortable predicament she'd been forced into.

No, he wasn't in love with Faith Roth.

He didn't count the hours until he'd see her again or have an overwhelming desire to write sappy odes or present her with flowers. Romantic claptrap was beyond him. Thank God.

That reminded Constantine that he never did speak with Harvey and find out why he urgently needed to see him. Come to think of it, Constantine hadn't seen Harvey since before Leopold told him Harvey was trying to find him.

He'd have to seek out his old friend when he returned to the manor house.

For now, his quest was to persuade Faith to stay in England as his amanuensis when their faux betrothal was officially broken. Of course, a substantial raise was in order, but would it be enough to compensate for the gossip that would follow, particularly if word spread that Faith still worked for him?

Would Constantine choose to do so if he were in her position?

The truth kicked him in the stomach.

Not for a thousand gold coins.

Which was likely why Faith had accepted the position as Mrs. Peagilly's traveling companion. They'd be gone a few months, maybe a year, and when Faith returned, only a few spiteful tabbies who had nothing else to think about would remember the broken betrothal.

Hellfire.

He really, *really* should've thought through all the possible consequences of agreeing to a fake engagement. Losing his amanuensis—the best he'd ever employed—was not among them.

Neither was Faith leaving the country for God only knew how long.

Settling beneath the oak's protective branches, she removed her bonnet, then pulled her knees to her chest and, in a winsome, childlike gesture, rested her chin atop them as she stared at the glorious tableau before her.

"It's pretty up here. Very peaceful." The rising sun created a perfect backdrop to her silhouette. "The view is as spectacular as you said."

As Constantine observed Faith, unpretentious and unspoiled, a crazy, outrageous, wholly implausible thought forged its way to the forefront of his mind.

Why not make the betrothal real—a marriage of convenience?

His mind stalled for a heartbeat, then accelerated with the possibility.

Yes. Yes. A marriage of convenience.

The very thing.

A perfect solution.

Giddiness gripped him, and he had to bite the inside of his cheek to hide his grin.

They worked well together. Faith wasn't a female who demanded fripperies, fallalls, entertaining, and his undivided attention. She was intelligent, sensible, pragmatic, and not given to swooning or hysterics. She didn't mind insects either.

In short, they were well-suited.

He permitted a minuscule upward tip of his mouth. Well-suited indeed.

There was no one else he'd rather marry, in truth.

No need for declarations of love and devotion and all of that sentimental twaddle. Emotions just mucked things up.

He found her desirable, and given her fervent responses to his kisses, she returned the feeling.

Respect, esteem, admiration, and desire.

Not a bad way to start a marriage of convenience.

He'd never considered marrying for love. Well, the truth of it was, he hadn't considered marriage much at all. As the third son, there really was no need.

Constantine would see to it that Faith wanted for nothing. If she desired—he very much hoped she would—she could continue as his scrivener. If she still wanted to travel, they could do so together and make it a scientific, sightseeing adventure.

The more he pondered the possibility, the more the idea grew on him. The trick would be to convince Faith that a match between them also benefited her. And he had bloody little time to do it in.

"Are you going to stand there staring at me in that serious, brooding fashion?" Faith's attention dipped to the basket as she removed her bonnet and laid it beside her. "I'm still hungry. You interrupted my breakfast."

"Forgive me." Constantine levered to the ground beside her and, after extending his legs and crossing his ankles, set the basket between them.

Faith promptly lifted the towel and laid it upon her gown before plucking a cinnamon bun from the basket.

Grinning, she took a large bite, then closed her eyes and groaned.

It took every ounce of his will, honor, and a severe admonition that he was a gentleman to not let his thoughts trundle down a dangerous and ungentlemanly path.

A sprinkle of cinnamon and sugar balanced on her lower lip.

Before he realized what he was about, Constantine bent and licked the speck away.

Her eyes flew open, and her lips parted.

Their eyes locked, a question in his and an answer in hers.

Slowly, he inched his mouth nearer and nearer to give Faith time to turn away or object.

She arched upward, closing the remaining inch, then looped her arms around his neck and opened her mouth to him.

She tasted of cinnamon and sugar; it was heady, intoxicating, and addicting.

Constantine wasn't aware of moving the basket aside, taking the towel and cinnamon bun from her lap, or laying Faith beside him. Every sense, every thought, was trained on the woman in his arms, kissing him with exuberance and hunger that was as welcome as it was unexpected.

One hand on her slender waist and the other cradling her against his chest, he rained kisses over her forehead, cheeks, eyes, chin, and then her lush, swollen mouth again. Passion and desire grew into a raging conflagration.

He must stop before he lost control.

With grudging reluctance, Constantine lifted his mouth from hers.

He would never dishonor Faith by taking her before they exchanged vows.

Faith's eyelashes fluttered, and she slowly opened her eyes. Passion and awe shone there.

"Are you trying to seduce me, Lord Constantine?"

Her voice emerged thick and sultry, and for an instant—only a very minute, insane instant—he considered tossing honor to the wind.

Faith wasn't the type of woman to relinquish her virtue without a ring on her finger.

"Mayhap." Chuckling, he waggled his eyebrows. "Is it working?"

"No." She elevated her eyebrows while giving him an arch look. "I have more sense than that."

More was the pity.

She sat up and, after adjusting her skirts into a semblance of respectability once more, rummaged through the basket before lifting an apple out. "Now, pray tell, why did you insist on joining me when you knew I wanted to be alone?"

Never one to mince words, Faith proceeded to take a bite from the apple.

"I don't want you to leave, Faith."

He took her free hand and balanced on one knee. Better seize the opportunity while he could.

"What... Constantine, what are you doing?"

Perceptibly flustered and her voice breathy, Faith seemed slightly panicked, and for a blink of her long lashes, he almost hesitated to proceed. Utterly flummoxed, she dropped the apple onto her lap and blinked so rapidly that she might've had a lash fall into her eye.

"Marry me, Faith. It's the perfect solution. Not only will it curb any gossip, but it also allows us to continue to work together."

Constantine cringed inwardly at how impersonal his proposal sounded. He was bloody awful at this sort of thing. Always had been. Pretty words and romantic phrases were as foreign to him as face paint and curling irons.

Eyes round pools of incredulous astonishment, Faith gaped at him, slack-mouthed.

For the first time in their acquaintance, Constantine had rendered her speechless.

He scrambled for other less mercenary reasons the match

benefited them both. Giving Faith's hand an encouraging squeeze, he forged onward with a new tact.

"We respect each other, and our kisses lead me to believe we'd suit in other areas too. You would have the family you've been denied, and your future would be secure with me. Finances would never be an issue for you either."

Probably too soon to mention bedding her.

"Are you...?" Her chest rose as she inhaled a deep breath and eyed him as if he'd turned pink and grown a spiral horn from his forehead. "Are you suggesting a marriage of... convenience with me?"

Her voice rising an octave on the last word ought to have warned Constantine, but the truth of it was, he was rather more nervous than he'd anticipated being. His heart bludgeoned his ribs, his blood careened along his veins like a runaway stallion, and a sharp rock jabbed mercilessly at his knee.

He nodded and raised her hand to his mouth.

"I am. Say yes, Faith. A match between us is not only logical and convenient, but it also solves so many problems."

"Prob-lems?" Faith sputtered, her eyes dual storm clouds as she jerked her hand away. "*Problems?*" She said again, this time more forcibly. She opened and closed her mouth twice before a choppy tirade of invectives tumbled forth.

"Of all the... I cannot believe... Beyond the pale... Infuriating... Who does he...? MY GOD!"

Not precisely the reaction Constantine had anticipated.

He was the son of a duke.

Faith was an orphan of questionable lineage.

A union between them was much more beneficial to her than to him. Didn't she understand that? Unless she harbored a romantic notion of falling in love, that was.

No. That was ludicrous.

Faith wasn't the sort of woman who'd appreciate syrupy sonnets or inflated displays of devotion. At least nothing in her comportment since they'd met suggested she was given to nonsensical fantasies about love.

Blast.

Constantine hadn't considered that possibility—a strategic error on his part.

"You arrogant, self-centered, dimwitted, clueless...*Oooh*!" Faith fisted her hands, and something very near a growl of frustrated anger hissed through her clenched teeth.

"We may come to feel affection for one another in time," he blundered onward, grasping at anything that might win her over. "My parents did..."

That had been the absolute wrong thing to say.

"No." Tears filled Faith's eyes as she frantically shook her head, causing several strawberry blonde curls to slip loose of their pins. "No."

She rose to her knees and hurled the apple like a miniature cannonball, hitting him in the middle of his chest.

"NO!"

The well of tears overflowed, spilling down her cheeks.

Her pain eviscerated Constantine, and he shifted to embrace and comfort her.

Her tears cleaved his heart, shredding the organ.

"Faith, what...?"

She shoved his chest with both hands, and Constantine toppled over, sprawling onto his back, arms still reaching for her.

Mouth pinched tight, she scrambled to her feet and stared down at him, fairly quivering with outrage. And hurt.

He was astute enough to recognize he'd wounded her. *Again.*

"I don't need your misplaced pity, nor do I want to be

convenient or the solution to your problems, my lord." She straightened her spine, rigid and unyielding as an iron bar, before thrusting out that stubborn chin. "Stay away from me until I leave the day after tomorrow."

A sob tried to escape, and Faith pressed a fist to her mouth. With that, she turned on her heels and darted down the hill.

Constantine let his arms flop to his sides.

Faith had refused him.

She didn't want to marry him.

By thunder, the ache in Constantine's chest hurt something bloody awful.

A curious rook hopped along a branch, peering down at him.

"If you're wise, old fellow, stay single. Females are simply impossible to understand."

NINETEEN

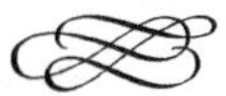

Forgive me, old chap, but I'll be on my way to London by the time you receive this. I tried to find you to tell you in person. I couldn't stay another day. I must declare myself to Aurelie.

I love her, and at least then I'll know where I stand. Never thought I'd find myself in this position, but love does strange things to a fellow. Perhaps someday you'll fall in love, and then you'll understand.

I borrowed a horse and shall stable it in your mews until I can arrange to return it to Dovetonwick Court. By the by, as I was leaving, I saw Martin speaking to a stable hand. I didn't hear the conversation except for Kellinggrave saying to make sure the coach was ready.

I'll see you in London. Wish me luck!

~Mr. Harvey Camberg-Trainer, in a short note
to Lord Constantine Kellinggrave

Lady Edyth's bedchamber
That evening—the much anticipated and touted ball

Faith stared at the elegant, composed woman gazing back at her in the cheval mirror. She touched the emerald and diamond earrings dangling from her earlobes, then the pendant nestled at the apex of her collarbone with her fingertip. It was amazing what a costly gown, lavish jewels, a touch of cosmetics, and a gifted hair stylist could do.

One could almost believe Faith had been born an aristocrat.

Formerly Lady Charlotte's, the emerald green gown trimmed in gold braid and lace Faith wore was, in a word, exquisite. She fingered the fine fabric, unable to believe the transformation that had taken place in her appearance over the past two hours.

"Oh, Faith," Edyth breathed, clasping her hands together. Eyes shining with approval, she circled Faith. "You are breathtaking. You're going to make those snitty gossips *sooo* jealous."

Glee filtered into her voice.

Wearing a white silk gown featuring a silver lace overskirt, Edyth appeared angelic with her blonde hair artfully arranged atop her head. Faith liked Constantine's youngest sister very much indeed. They might've become good friends had circumstances been different.

Nita adjusted the gown's hem before standing back, satisfied.

"Better than I had anticipated, Miss Roth."

"Nita, you are a miracle worker."

Faith turned and embraced the startled servant.

Blushing, Nita shook her head.

"No, Miss. I knew you'd be dazzling in the gown with your coloring." With a final pleased glance, she made for the door. "Excuse me. I still need to check on Lady Charlotte and the duchess one final time."

Never had Faith anticipated attending such a touted affair, dressed like a *haut ton* denizen. Some might say she was mutton dressed as lamb, and perhaps she was. Nevertheless, tonight, she was an honored guest of the Duke and Duchess of Landrith and, to all and sundry until the day after tomorrow, their youngest son's betrothed.

Yes, it was the stuff of which fairytales were made, but even pragmatic spectacle-wearing wallflower scriveners were entitled to a night of frivolous fantasies. The real world would return tomorrow with its harsh, uncompromising realities. But reality couldn't snatch her memories. Memories she'd cherish into her old age as a spinster with a dog and a cat and maybe a bird.

She'd recall the Landriths' house party, the extravagant ball, and Constantine when she was morose or having a fit of the blue devils. The man who'd somehow taken her heart captive without her being aware.

Once Nita had gone, Lady Edyth grabbed Faith's hands and, laughing, spun her in a wide circle. "I vow Constantine will regret the day he let you get away."

He might regret a marriage of convenience with her hadn't come to fruition but naught else.

"As we were never really betrothed, I sincerely doubt that." Faith softened her response with a warm smile.

Constantine had to be the most unromantic dolt she'd ever known.

Would any woman be thrilled at being the solution to a man's problems?

In truth, yes. Yes, they would.

The very nature of arranged marriages and marriages of

convenience were mutually beneficial business arrangements that often solved a problem for one or both parties.

Faith had overreacted to Constantine's ill-thought-out, detached proposal. Once she'd calmed down and had time to ponder her emotional response, that had become crystal clear. That admission brought no small amount of self-castigation and heaped more chagrin on her already humiliated soul.

Nevertheless, she didn't shy away from examining *why* she'd responded as drastically as she had.

The answer had blindsided her, striking her so forcefully and unexpectedly that she'd collapsed onto Lady Edyth's bed. Staring up at the sky-blue pleated canopy, a parade of recollections traipsed across her mind.

She'd done the untenable, the very thing she'd vowed to eschew—she'd fallen in love with her aristocratic employer.

Ooh, the heart was a traitorous, feckless organ.

If Constantine had hinted that he held her in any affection, she might've been tempted to consider his offer. Her heart had screamed, "Yes! Yes, I'll marry you."

But Faith's common sense, her cautious self, had flinched with each plausible reason he gave for them to marry.

She knew he was a logical, practical, confounding man.

Lord, how well she knew it.

It shouldn't have surprised her that he'd approach marriage with the same pragmatism and rationale he did all else. What did surprise her was that he'd choose her. And that brought her full circle to the irrefutable fact that he valued her amanuensis skills far more than he did her.

Lady Edyth sobered, her earlier radiance fading.

"I wish you could be my sister, Faith. I adore Charlotte, of course, but she's sixteen years older than me. I know she loves me, but she's always been more like a second mother than a sister—a confidant and friend."

"I'm several years older too," Faith reminded her as she collected her white satin elbow-length gloves.

"Yes, but I feel like I've always known you." Lady Edyth's pretty green eyes grew misty. "And you're going away, and I shall probably never see you again. And Charlotte is going away, and it will just be me in this big house. My brothers will return to their lives, and I shall have no one."

Faith gathered her into her arms.

"We can write, and there is no reason why we cannot see one another when I am in England."

Actually, there was a six foot two, jade-eyed reason.

"Do you promise?" Lady Edyth pulled back and searched Faith's face.

There was always the risk Faith would run into Constantine, but what this young girl asked was within her scope to make her happy.

"I promise, Edyth."

A glance at the white marble bedside clock revealed it was time to go below.

Faith's stomach roiled at the thought of seeing Constantine after this morning. But she wasn't a coward. She would face this evening with the graciousness and eloquence she'd been taught.

She would do Hester Shepherd proud.

"Wait." Lady Edyth rushed to her dressing table. She seized a crystal perfume jar. "It's only heliotrope *eau de toilette*. Mama says I'm too young for perfume, but this is my favorite scent."

She removed the stopper and dabbed her inner wrist and behind each ear. Afterward, she passed it to Faith, who did the same.

Once Faith pulled on her gloves, she took a final glance in the mirror.

A confident, regal woman stared back at her. A woman who was perfectly capable of going below, holding her head up, and cocking a snook at those who looked down their pretentious noses at her. More on point, she was strong and capable, and any encounters with Constantine she would handle with grace and aplomb.

"Shall we go?" She extended her elbow.

"Indeed." Eyes sparkling with excitement, Lady Edyth slipped her hand into the crook of Faith's elbow. "This is my first formal ball. Do you think I'll dance every dance?"

The lovely girl would have the young bucks eating out of her hand.

"I have no doubt you will." Already a beauty on the cusp of womanhood, the girl's kind heart and generous spirit were certain to make her a favorite among the *ton*. They might also make her a target of the waspish-tongued, envious wallflowers.

Edyth gave her an uncertain, sideways look as they went below.

"Will you dance with Constantine?"

Faith had considered that since running back to the house.

If he asked, she must accept because to refuse meant she'd have to sit out every dance for the rest of the evening. And by Jupiter, as this was likely the only *le beau monde* ball she'd ever attend, and she'd probably never wear anything as marvelous as this gown and these borrowed jewels again, she meant to put aside her concerns and enjoy herself for a few hours.

"I shall."

For in two days, she'd start a new chapter of her life and leave the man who had captured her heart as easily as netting a Holly Blue.

TWENTY

*I've eloped to Gretna Green with Martin Kellinggrave.
Don't try to stop me, for I've already been compromised
and may well carry his child. Mama and Papa think he is
a fortune hunter, but I know Martin loves me. No man
can be as solicitous and tender as he if he didn't truly
love me.*

*I shall contact you when I return from my honeymoon.
Forgive me for putting the burden of telling our parents on
your shoulders. I know they will take it better coming
from you.*

~Miss Adelle Breadalbane, in a short note
to her sister, Miss Amelia Breadalbane

Dovetonwick Court ballroom
Ten minutes later

Taking a swift glance around the ballroom, Constantine braced himself for a glimpse of Faith. His initial perusal revealed she hadn't come down yet. His mother caught his eye, and with an almost imperceptible nudge of her chin and flare of her eyes, she called him to her side.

Harvey had succumbed to his love for the enchanting Aurelie Allemand and had hightailed it for London last night. Berkham had delivered the short note to Constantine when he'd returned to the house this morning.

As Constantine wended his way through the milling guests—at least a hundred more had arrived for the Landriths' ostentatious ball—he smiled and acted the congenial gentleman.

Everyone believed Constantine was the austere, logical, serious brother by choice or perhaps by God-given design.

Nothing could be farther from the truth.

Leopold, the heir, was the golden child—talented at everything from shooting to singing, responsible, loyal, and reliable. Cedric, the spare, was carefree, adventuresome, daring, and the jester of the family. That left Constantine to fill the only available slot: the practical, intelligent, religious, *boring* brother.

Except he learned he wasn't cut out for the cloth, mainly because he couldn't bear the hypocrisy of not only those who filled the pews each Sunday but those in church leadership who exploited their power and position. Nor could he abide the female parishioners who hinted they wouldn't be opposed to unholy assignations with him.

Not every man of God was dishonest, compromised, or a counterfeit. Wilfred Howerton was as sincere a vicar as Constantine had ever met—decent down to the marrow in his bones.

Simply put, Constantine's temperament had rendered him unfit for religious service.

He liked adventures too, his musical talents were on par with Leo's, and he possessed a playful nature to rival Cedric's, if anyone had cared to notice.

"Mother. You look exceptionally lovely this evening."

He kissed her cheek, and she looped her arm in his and led him to a quiet corner. Not that two hundred animated guests, a five-piece stringed orchestra, and a score of attentive servants scurrying hither and yon permitted any genuine quiet space in the ballroom.

"I'm worried about you, Constantine." Mother put her palm to his cheek. "You care for that girl."

No need to ask what girl she referred to.

"More, I think, than you've even admitted to yourself, son."

Gazing out over the merry-makers, he marshaled a rueful smile.

"I asked her to marry me today." More fool he. "Even got down on one knee."

The last emerged far more cryptic and sardonic than he'd intended.

"*You* did?" Surprise rounded her eyes before they narrowed with keen comprehension.

Leave it to Mother to discern there was more to the story.

"But...?"

Linking his hands behind him, Constantine rocked back on his heels and pointed his gaze to the ornate plasterwork, crown molding, and cornices gracing the ceiling.

"I botched it rather badly." He winced at the memory. "I suggested a marriage of convenience would solve our problems."

"Oh, darling. Please say you didn't." He heard the grimace in her voice as she placed her hand on his shoulder in a gesture meant to comfort.

He didn't deserve comfort, however.

Constantine heaved a defeated sigh and dragged his attention back to his mother.

Consternation shone in her eyes.

"In point of fact, I did. Let's just say my ineptness was not well-received."

"Hmm, perhaps you might try something a trifle more romantic next time?"

A glint of humor replaced her dismay.

"Next time?" He scuffed the toe of his shoe on the floor, regret bludgeoning his heart. "There won't be a next time, I'm afraid. Faith is leaving in two days."

"Pshaw. You're a scientist, Constantine." A twinkle entered her eyes, now filled with maternal affection and pride. "Do you give up the first time when conducting an experiment or research when the results are not what you wished or hoped for?"

No. He certainly did not. He took a different approach. Over and over until he found what worked. But that took time, and he didn't have time.

True, but he did have tonight and tomorrow.

The minuet ended, and after bowing and curtsying, the couples ambled from the dance floor.

Holding a glass of champagne, Leopold chatted with Father and a couple of the duke's cronies. He spied their mother in deep conversation with Constantine and cocked an eyebrow as if to say, *Glad it's you and not me, old chap.*

Face flushed and appearing wholly vexed, Uncle Hayward plowed his way through the throng toward Father, unceremoniously shoving guests out of the way. His rudeness earned him several scowls, and not a few muttered reprimands.

He seemed uncharacteristically frazzled and didn't even offer Lady Wortley-Titherton an apology when his pumping elbow jabbed her arm, causing her to splash champagne down her well-endowed, violet silk-covered bosom.

Her strangled shriek of outrage paled in comparison to Miss Looram's when Uncle accidentally tripped Mr. Neville Dempsey, Wilfred Howerton's shy and awkward curate. Flapping his arms like a stork about to take flight, the unlucky fellow took the flailing and screeching Miss Looram to the floor with him, landing atop her.

Several guests, including Howerton and Charlotte, rushed to assist them.

Across the ballroom, Cedric dissolved into laughter at the spectacle, his shoulders shaking so hard that he dashed out the open terrace doors.

"Constantine, pay attention."

His mother whacked his shoulder with her fan—this one a gold and ivory lace affair.

Just how many fans did Mother own?

For her not to notice the commotion across the dance floor meant she was good and truly absorbed in his dilemma.

"Yes, Mother?"

"I've seen how you and Miss Roth look at each other when you think the other isn't looking. Love is different for everyone, dear. Don't discount your feelings because they don't mimic what you've seen others experience."

That was exactly what he'd done.

Convinced himself he didn't love Faith because he wasn't a mopey, confused mess like Harvey or giddy as a grig, a perpetually grinning sot like Brockman.

What Faith made Constantine feel defied description. Words were inadequate, especially for a man not eloquent with words.

She made him a better person. Everything seemed more

vibrant and intense when Faith was near. She invoked deep abiding contentment and filled his soul with joy.

And he wanted to be with her, day and night, in every situation. Wanted to share his thoughts, ideas, dreams, and worries just to hear her voice and see her eyes alight with excitement or soften with compassion.

If that wasn't love, he didn't know what was.

He, Lord Constantine Peyton Harland Kellinggrave, loved the impossible, obstinate, clever, witty, beautiful, maddening as Hades Faith Roth.

Stupid dolt.

That was what he should have told her before he proposed except, perhaps, not the maddening as Hades bit.

"Miss Roth just entered the ballroom." Mother gave him a little shove. "Now go. Put that brilliant mind to work and find a way to win that young woman. I should very much like her as a daughter-in-law."

"I'll see what I can do." Constantine gave her a swift hug.

Faith, so breathtakingly stunning that his breath hitched in his lungs, glided across the ballroom, seemingly on air. She hadn't seen him yet, so he took a few moments to appreciate each of her precious features.

The heart was a queer thing.

What he'd believed was aggravation and frustration toward her had actually been him fighting against the attraction he felt.

Fearful that she'd bolt and run, Constantine approached her as cautiously as he would a nervous doe.

Edyth saw him first and winked, the precocious minx.

"Faith?"

She stiffened, and he could see her erecting her battlements as she pivoted in his direction.

"Oh, my. Something seems to have happened." Edyth

stared at a weeping Ida Looram being led from the ballroom by her mother and sister before she switched her focus to Charlotte's pale face. "Charlotte looks rather upset. I must see if I can help."

In a trice, she'd disappeared into the crowd.

"Good evening, my lord." Faith stared past his shoulder.

Mother gave an imperial wave of her hand, and the orchestra immediately launched into a waltz. Of course, it was a waltz, no doubt at the duchess's behest.

Constantine didn't mind her interference if it meant aiding his cause in winning Faith.

Wilfred and a couple of chaps escorted a beet-faced Mr. Dempsey to the punch bowl. The mortified curate downed two glasses of punch without taking a breath.

Edyth emerged from the crowd and wrapped an arm around Charlotte's waist, saying something in her ear that caused Charlotte to chuckle and hug Edyth.

Despite being so much younger than the rest of the Kellinggrave children, ever since Edyth learned to talk, she'd always been the peacemaker and soother.

"I know I deserve your contempt after this morning, Faith. Regardless, more than anything in the world, I wish to make amends for my callousness and insensitivity." He held out his hand. "Would you honor me with this dance?"

Her gaze remained fixated on his gloved hand for five seconds, and he fervently prayed she'd say yes.

Her gaze crept up his chest, past his chin, and she met his eyes.

Their gazes meshed, and the world tipped on its axis.

She tipped his world on its axis.

Her bowed mouth swept upward into a ghost of a smile.

"You know I cannot refuse lest I sit out the rest of the dances, which I am loath to do."

He grinned as she placed her hand atop his and permitted him to escort her onto the chalked floor. Bending his neck, he spoke into her ear. "You are utterly ravishing. A vision."

The emerald gown and jewels were stunning, but *she* was magnificent. Her glorious hair had been swept into a Grecian style, and it shimmered as if spun with copper and gold threads.

Pink tinged Faith's cheeks. "You look rather splendid yourself."

Constantine chose a spot on the edge of the dance floor near the open French windows. He hoped to whisk Faith outside and beg for her forgiveness. He wasn't above groveling. In that respect, mayhap he wasn't so different from Harvey after all.

Faith curtsied, and he bowed, and then she was in his arms. She kept her gaze fixed on his chin as he swept her around the floor.

"Did Embly miss a spot?"

"What?" Her chocolatey gaze flew to his. "I don't..."

Giving her his most charming grin, Constantine drew her closer.

"You were staring at my chin, Faith."

"Oh."

Pressing his palm to the small of her back, he lowered his head until his mouth touched her hair. Unable to resist, he touched lips to her crown.

She stiffened but didn't pull away.

Encouraged, he kissed her hair again, not caring who bloody well saw. For tonight, she was his betrothed, and he blasted well intended to act like a man wholly besotted.

Because he was.

The essences of rose, heliotrope, and bergamot surrounded him—a heady aphrodisiac— though he was positive she hadn't meant the delicate fragrance to have that effect.

"I'm terribly sorry, my precious love," he whispered. "I vow I didn't mean to hurt you. Forgive me."

Faith missed a step, her confused gaze seeking his. "I…"

"Shh, don't say anything. Not yet. Let me explain first. Please."

She cast a covert glance around. "We're being watched."

Constantine had expected as much. He shifted his attention to scan the room.

Mother stood to the side, keenly observing him, a pleased smile bending her lightly rouged mouth. She veered her gaze toward the open doors, swung her focus to Faith, then pointedly to the doors again. Eyebrows peaked, she silently shouted across the room.

Take her outside.

Not exactly subtle.

Mother was actually encouraging him to sweep Faith onto the terrace.

Always a dutiful son, Constantine obliged with the next wide turn of the dance.

"What are you doing?" Faith hissed beneath her breath, digging her heels in and refusing to budge. She sent a nervous, furtive glance around. "I agreed to a dance, not a clandestine meeting."

"We'll dance out here, in full view of those on the terrace and in the ballroom, but I intend to have my say."

The night was cool, but not uncomfortably so. As they had the other night, lanterns on the terrace and strategically placed in the small gardens provided muted light. The glowing orbs also added a romantic element and even a hint of mystery.

She elevated a skeptical eyebrow. "Didn't you do that this morning?"

"I made an arse of myself this morning." Constantine drew her into his arms once more, reveling in the wonder that was this woman.

Faith didn't resist, but neither did she look enthusiastic.

"Yes, you did," she agreed with a sniff. "You have until the end of this dance, Lord Constantine, to say what you will. Then I'm going inside and avoiding you for the rest of the evening."

Hurt trickled into her last words, rendering them slightly husky.

He tipped her chin upward, losing himself in the mesmerizing pools of her eyes. He wasn't a man proficient at flowery phrases, but he could say the words that mattered.

"I love you, Faith."

She stopped, peering up at him, hope and wonder and disbelief skittering across the delicate planes of her face. In typical Faith fashion, she did the unexpected.

Grasping his hand, she looked this way, then that, and then hauled him to a dark nook between a potted pear tree in the corner of the terrace, out of sight of prying eyes.

"Now, what did you say?"

Constantine couldn't help it. He chuckled and cupped her face with his hands.

"I love you, Faith Roth."

"You truly love me?" Awe made her tone soft with wonderment.

"I do." He kissed her nose. "I really, truly do, my darling."

"Why?" Suspicion furrowed her forehead.

Why?

How could he possibly list the myriad of reasons?

"Because, my darling, I cannot imagine a life without you in it. It would be shallow and empty and incomplete. My greatest desire is to fall asleep with you in my arms, and for you to be the first thing I see when I open my eyes each morning."

She fingered his starched neckcloth, a small smile playing around the edges of her pink mouth. "So no marriage of convenience?"

The incorrigible vixen.

Was there any other woman like Faith Roth?

No, thank God.

"No marriage of convenience, sweetheart. But a love match, for I hope, my dearest heart, that you love me too."

She broke into a radiant smile, then stood up on her toes to kiss Constantine full on the mouth, sending blood scorching through his veins.

"I think it's quite convenient," she said, her voice husky, "that not only do we love each other, but we are already betrothed."

Capturing her in his embrace, he growled into her ear, "I'd prefer a short betrothal. Very short."

Unable to resist, he nipped her earlobe.

Faith gasped.

"Short is good." Her voice came out a throaty purr. "Excellent, in fact."

He nuzzled her neck. "I propose an extended honeymoon, beginning in the Mediterranean, darling."

"Perfect. But only after Joy Morrisette's soirée. I've already promised to attend." Faith grasped his lapels. "Now kiss me properly."

Constantine was only too happy to oblige.

EPILOGUE

*Once again, I must beg your forgiveness, my friend.
Aurelie said yes. We are honeymooning in France. Her
grandparents and an older sister and her family still live
there. I shall return the first week in October. Of course, I'll
understand if you have dismissed me.*

*Nonetheless, I cannot regret taking a chance at love.
Other things come and go, but true love lasts forever. May
you someday find the same happiness as I have.*

~Harvey Camberg-Trainer, in a letter
to Lord Constantine Kellinggrave

Mayfair, London
Morrisettes' drawing room
27 September 1818

Yes, married life suited Faith. Suited her very much indeed,
though it had only been ten glorious days since she and

Constantine had exchanged vows in Dovetonwick Court's drawing room surrounded by his immediate family. Now they were her family, and they had taken her into their fold with such kindness and warmth that it still made her eyes misty.

Neither she nor Constantine had wanted to wait for the banns to be read, so the Duke of Landrith had used his influence to procure a special license.

Faith sent a surreptitious glance around the hospitable drawing room. A successful physician from a noble family, Dr. Morrisette and his wife, Joy, preferred simplicity and functionality.

The other branch of the Kellinggraves had departed in a huff before the ball ended. Hayward Kellinggrave blamed the duke for Martin eloping with sixteen-year-old Adelle Breadalbane.

Good Lord, there had been a colossal dust-up when the elopement news became known. Any residual gossip still whispered into eager ears about Faith and Constantine instantly ceased. There was a much bigger scandal to bandy about.

Constantine explained that Martin was in debt up to his bloodshot eyeballs, and the Duke of Landrith had refused to pay his debts again. So desperate and facing debtors' prison, Martin had turned his licentious designs on the inexperienced and empty-headed Miss Breadalbane, seduced the chit, and then hied her off to Gretna Green.

"I'd wager the greedy, unscrupulous bounder abandons the silly girl the moment he gets his hands on her fortune," Constantine said.

Faith felt sorry for Adelle, even if the girl had started rumors that Faith was Constantine's mistress. Adelle had made an abominable choice that would plague her for the rest of her life.

Turning to Trinity Ablethorne, Faith said, "If you are

interested, I know a delightful woman seeking a traveling companion. I had agreed to take the position before Constantine proposed to me. We are joining her on a trip to the Mediterranean next month."

Trinity's countenance lit up, and she gave an excited nod.

"I would be very interested. My current employer is a dear lady, but she spends the majority of her time in the chapel or sleeping. I am quite bored. I thought I'd enjoy staying in England, but it seems I've developed a bit of a wanderer's heart."

"Excellent." Faith lifted her blue rose teacup. "I took the liberty of telling Mrs. Peagilly I knew someone with extensive experience as a traveling companion. She said she'd be delighted to meet you. I believe you shall get on famously." After taking a sip of excellent oolong tea, she said, "I shall give you her direction, and you can write her."

Trinity smiled, her pale, hydrangea-blue eyes sparkling. "I shall do so as soon as I return home."

Feeling Constantine's heated gaze upon her, Faith lifted her head.

No one had ever told her that soul mates could speak with their eyes or reach across a room and caress each other with a sweep of their gaze.

Love was a glorious, mysterious, all-consuming paradox.

She met his eyes from where he stood, talking with Dr. Morrisette, Ronan Brockman, and Theran Rutland. The smoldering glint in his hooded gaze caused dual paths of heat to skate up her cheeks. No doubt he, too, remembered this morning.

It had been a most invigorating start to the day.

From beside her on the settee, Mrs. Shepherd, attired in her signature dove gray and black striped ensemble, touched Faith's arm. "Might I have a word with Faith in private?"

The other ladies graciously murmured their consent and left Mrs. Shepherd and Faith alone.

Her expression serious enough to cause Faith's nape hair to rise, Mrs. Shepherd patted her hand reassuringly.

"Is something wrong, Mrs. Shepherd?"

"No need to fret. I presume you read the letter I sent cautioning you to have nothing to do with Aloysius Petheringham?"

"I did." Faith nodded and set her teacup down. The china rattled in the saucer, the only indication the conversation disturbed her. She puzzled her forehead as she recalled reading the troubling letter. "He never contacted me, however."

Mrs. Shepherd's mouth tightened, disapproval stamped upon her features. "That's because the blackguard was arrested for abducting you as a child."

"Pardon?" Faith felt the blood drain from her face and pool in the soles of her feet. At this moment, if she stood, she'd fall flat on her face.

She'd been abducted?

Why?

Who was she?

Where was her family? *Who* was her family?

The questions came one after another, careening around in her head and bouncing off her skull with such intensity she felt momentarily light-headed.

Who am I?

Constantine must've seen her distress, for he excused himself from his friends and came to sit beside her. He took her hand in his, lending her his strength and comfort. At his touch, peace shrouded her. Everything would be all right.

"I'm right here, my love."

How Faith adored him. She searched his eyes. "Did you know?"

"No, he did not." Compassion etched Mrs. Shepherd's lined face. "You see, my dear, Petheringham is your stepbrother and the man who called himself John Smith. He brought you to Haven House and Academy for the Enrichment of Young Women."

Shock rendered Faith speechless. She'd anticipated what Mrs. Shepherd might reveal, but it certainly wasn't that her stepbrother had abducted her.

"He was after the fortune and believed with you out of the way, as the eldest surviving stepsibling, the funds would transfer to him."

"Fortune?" Faith shook her head.

"Substantial fortune thanks to wise investments of the trustees," Mrs. Shepherd said.

"I'm so confused." Faith hated that her voice trembled.

"Yes, it is quite a lot to take in." Mrs. Shepherd exchanged a speaking glance with Constantine. "But you should know the whole of it. That is if you are up to it."

"By all means." Faith would know at last who she was.

Constantine linked his fingers with hers.

"Your given name is Bernadette Rennison, and you were left a fortune in trust by your grandfather, Chadwick Fernsby, Viscount Aberforth."

"My grandfather was a viscount?"

An understanding, if somewhat indulgent, smile warmed Mrs. Shepherd's face. "Indeed, and your mother was his only child. A nephew, I believe, inherited the viscountcy and all of the entailed property. Lord Aberforth's personal fortune he bequeathed to you."

"Not his daughter?" Constantine asked.

Shrugging, Mrs. Shepherd flicked a Shrewsbury biscuit crumb from her lap. "I can only speculate that he didn't approve of your mother's choice of husbands."

"Your mother remarried, acquiring two stepsons and a stepdaughter, each much older than you. Widowed a second time, she passed away six months after Mr. Petheringham, leaving you, a mere toddler, alone in the world. Aloysius Petheringham—the eldest of your three step-siblings—thought to steal your inheritance. It appears your other stepsiblings were unaware of their brother's perfidy."

Mrs. Shepherd's censorious sniff relayed what she thought of the scoundrel. "For the past two decades, he's been attempting to access the funds without success."

"How is it that he came to be arrested?" Faith asked, her mind reeling with the confounding information.

Mrs. Shepherd swiftly told them of her suspicions all those years ago, Petheringham's unnerving letters, his demands to know Faith's whereabouts, and how the investigator Mrs. Shepherd had recently hired uncovered information that suggested Petheringham wanted Faith—Bernadette—declared dead.

"I feared for your safety and have regretted I wasn't more suspicious of him from the beginning." Remorse shadowed the corners of Mrs. Shepherd's face. "There've been so many girls over the years that perhaps I've grown immune to the depths of wickedness and depravity mankind will sink to."

Faith covered her hand with her own. "Do not berate yourself, Mrs. Shepherd. Were it not for you, from what you have told me, I most likely would not be alive today, though why Petheringham didn't dispose of me from the onset makes no sense."

"He probably erroneously believed your disappearance was grounds enough to have you declared dead." Smirking, Constantine rubbed an eyebrow. "He sounds like a rather stupid fellow."

"You might be correct about that," Mrs. Shepherd agreed.

"Nevertheless, I cannot help but wonder if he also had his hand in Mrs. Petheringham's demise so conveniently soon after her husband's."

Faith's stomach churned at the possibility.

As if sensing her upset, Constantine drew her closer and whispered in her ear. "He cannot hurt you now, darling."

She smiled into his eyes.

"I will reimburse you for the cost of the investigator, Mrs. Shepherd." Constantine's features hardened into steely lines. "Your shrewdness may very well have saved my wife's life. I'm confident other charges will be brought against the blackguard as well. He'll never see the outside of a prison cell again if I have my way."

Faith hoped that was the case, but now that she was married, she needn't fret. Constantine would keep her safe.

"Perhaps, or perchance all of what transpired was part of the Lord's plan." Mrs. Shepherd pointed her gaze upward. "His ways are not our ways."

"If you'll excuse me, I wanted a word with Chasity." She rose and wended among the guests to where Chasity stood, chatting with Joy, Mercy, and Trinity.

Constantine leaned against the settee, putting one arm around Faith's shoulders and drawing little figure eights on the back of Faith's hand with the forefinger of his other hand.

"So, I've married myself an heiress and a blueblood to boot."

She scrunched her nose as she relaxed into the curve of his arm. "You know wealth, titles, and position have never mattered to me. They obviously don't matter to you either, or you'd never have married me."

He tilted her head upward until their gazes fused. Grazing his thumb over her jaw, he murmured, "We can deal with all of those details later. All that matters, now and forever, is that we are together."

Constantine's penetrating gaze caused Faith's blood to sing and left her slightly dizzy. This man was her everything. She'd follow him to the ends of the earth just to be able to show him how much she loved him until the days God had appointed them came to an end.

"Yes," she whispered, her focus straying to his molded mouth. "Forever and always, my love. Forever and always."

And then, because neither cared a jot about what was acceptable in polite drawing rooms, they sealed those reverent vows with a kiss.

If you'd like to leave a review, I would be grateful.

Keep reading for a free preview of
LADY TEMPTS A ROGUE
Secrets of Scandalous Ladies, Book Six

LADY TEMPTS A ROGUE
Secrets of Scandalous Ladies
Book 6

*Life is an unpredictable, mysterious journey, is it not?
After having spent several years traveling with Mrs.
Westcott, I vowed I would remain in England thereafter.
Convinced that I had seen and experienced all that any
soul could desire, I was committed to putting down roots
and settling into a comfortable, predictable life.*

*And yet, within a few short months in my most recent
position as a companion to an elderly dame who was
content to stay home except for attending church, I became
so restless, bored, and malcontented that I leaped—yes, very
nearly leaped about, clapping my hands, and giggling as if
I was queer in the attic—when the opportunity presented
itself to travel once again.*

*Tomorrow night, I set sail for the Mediterranean as a
companion to Mrs. Eustacia Peagilly. I do not know when*

I shall return to England, but I promise to write as I have always done. Do remember me in your prayers, for Mrs. Peagilly, despite her advanced years, is a bold adventurer at heart, and I expect many exciting challenges in the months ahead.

~Miss Trinity Ablethorne, in a letter
to her girlhood friend,
Mrs. Purity Mayfield-Rutland

19 October 1818
Daunting Duchess's foredeck
Ten minutes past nine P.M.

Here I go again, off to who knows where and for God only knows how long.

The tiniest pang of regret tightened Trinity's throat and cinched her heart before she squared her shoulders, lifted her chin, and pressed her lips into a firm line. *No regrets.* This life of adventure, possible peril, and assured excitement was far better than the mundane, safe, and secure—*boring as Hades*—existence of the past few months.

Perhaps she would have been contented if she were married and had a family...

No. Stop.

Stomping a foot, she gave one sharp shake of her head to dispel *that* wayward thought. At nearly six and twenty, the quixotic but impractical girlhood dream of a husband, four children (two boys and two girls), and a cozy cottage at the shore had been shoved far back on a cupboard shelf. The door had been firmly shut and the key turned in the lock, then tucked away so that temptation would not lure her into peeking inside from time to time to see what might have been.

This was her life, and she had a straightforward choice: to accept her fate or bemoan it.

Practical, resilient, and intrepid, Trinity chose the former.

Come, she chided herself, always one to face self-pity and discouragement with logic and stoicism.

You have much for which to be grateful.

How many women of humble origins have traveled as extensively as you?

Have eaten the rich, tantalizing foods of many cultures?

Have laughed (and also gasped) half in awe and half in astonishment at foreign entertainment and unique customs?

A gull landed on a nearby piling. Head cocked, the gray and white creature observed the tumult aboard the ship and then turned its tiny, black button eyes on her. The wind ruffled the bird's tail feathers, and it flapped its wings twice.

"Shouldn't you be tucked snuggly in your nest?" she asked the inquisitive bird. "Or wherever birds of your kind sleep?"

The gull flapped its wings again and took flight, circling above her once before gliding toward the chimney stacks a few streets away.

Pulling the hood of her serviceable woolen cloak farther over her head to prevent the breeze nipping at her cheeks from making her ears ache, Trinity scanned her gaze over the scruffy crew bustling about the deck with practiced skill before shifting her regard to the much less active East India Docks below.

This time of night, the wharf was vacant except for a trio of loudly singing, obviously pished sailors, a pair of scantily attired ladies of the evening—both revealing a shocking display of bare legs and voluptuous bosoms—and a tired appearing fellow, knitted hat pulled low over his forehead as he hunched into his jacket and lumbered down the long expanse.

From somewhere nearby, bawdy laughter, the lively strains of a fiddle, and more slurred singing carried seaward on the tangy river breeze.

Cleaner and less malodorous than several of the other docks Trinity had visited over the years, the East India Docks' pungent odors would, nevertheless, put off a less stalwart female.

Many a *beau monde* dandy too, she would wager.

The recipient of raw sewage and other equally noxious substances, the River Thames reeked to high heaven. Not enough to compel Trinity to cover her nose with her crochet-edged and lemon-water-scented handkerchief tucked into her inside cloak pocket but enough to prevent her from totally filling her lungs with the fetid air.

Realizing that she held each breath a second or two, Trinity released her current partial lungful in a small whoosh that created a miniature vapor cloud. Making a rueful face, she chuckled at her silliness. Sailing in October wasn't ideal, but she'd spend the winter in warmer climes, and that was much preferable to England's drizzly, bone-penetrating dampness.

At the docks' far end, a rickety hackney drawn by a sway-backed horse trundled along the cobbles, its wheels echoing hollowly in the gray, fog-shrouded atmosphere. A black cat darted in front of the coach, its tail pointed straight as it fled an invisible foe.

Not superstitious or given to frightening easily, Trinity nevertheless could not stave off the shudder scuttling from her waist to her nape and then padding across her shoulders like a kitten tiptoeing on a prickly bush.

A premonition?

Of what?

A deckhand yelling an ear-burning curse dragged her attention back to the commotion around her.

A wry grin pulled her mouth upward at the sides.

These past years, she had acquired knowledge of vulgar vocabulary that would cause Mrs. Hester Shepherd, the proprietress of the foundling home and school where Trinity had spent her childhood, to blush crimson.

Having been raised to be a proper lady, Trinity had never let such uncouth expletives pass her lips. But should she ever require a hardy curse guaranteed to make one's ears burn, she could summon several creative and physically impossible expletives with no effort whatsoever.

That she did not understand what half of them meant was of no consequence.

The *Daunting Duchess*—such a regal name for a rather nondescript frigate—sailed in less than an hour at high water.

Trinity's attention drifted toward the dock.

Odd that the captain had not ordered the gangway removed yet.

Weren't all the passengers aboard?

A tendril of hair that had escaped her neat chignon tickled her cheek.

Frowning, she brushed it aside.

Late this afternoon, when she and Mrs. Peagilly—presently enjoying a cup of ginger tea to stave off seasickness—boarded the vessel, Captain Horatio Breckett mentioned that seven other passengers also sailed to Morocco.

Trinity's girlhood friend, Faith Kellinggrave, and her new husband, Lord Constantine, were to have voyaged on the ship too. Unfortunately, Lord Constantine's father, the Duke of Landrith, had suffered a serious riding accident, causing the postponement of Faith's wedding trip until he recovered.

Besides two businessmen, Amos Truman-Shelton and

Lawrence Meriwether, Trinity had met the diplomat, Sir Godfrey McKinnick, his wife, Martha, and their two freckle-faced children, Gladys and Georgie—a thumb-sucking little chap still in short pants.

That left one passenger unaccounted for, though they might've boarded before Trinity and Mrs. Peagilly and, if a poor sailor, tucked themselves into their berth for what might be an unpleasant day or two or three.

Trinity had suffered horrid malaise on her first ocean voyage, but never again, thank God. Such was not the case for everyone, and she was most grateful her body had somehow adjusted to the sea's churning and bobbing so that sickness never afflicted her again. She'd truly thought she would die those first several hours and pitied those suffering seasickness for days on each voyage.

Earlier, when Mrs. Peagilly assured Trinity she could spare her company, her employer had also vowed that as long as she drank ginger tea, she would not succumb to nausea.

Trinity glanced to where the full moon hung in the sky, but given the almost eerily fine mist shrouding the horizon, the distant orb only managed a faint, silvery glow. The captain must be confident the haze would lift or, at the very least, disperse as they headed out to sea.

Trinity certainly hoped so.

She did not want the rolling fog to steal her last view of England's shoreline or obstruct the glittering stars above. The nocturnal lights appeared much more vivid and ever so much closer over the ocean than on land.

She'd always considered celestial navigation an extraordinary skill. Had she been a man, she might've pursued a life at sea. Years ago, she had borrowed a book from Glen Furrows, the sailing master on the *Liberty June,* about navigation using the stars. Scrunching her nose, she tried to recall the thin tome's title, but memory failed her.

Hunched into her wrap, a comfortable Kersey woolen shield against the evening's permeating chill, she staunchly determined not to go below until England's shoreline disappeared—which might be far sooner than she liked given the uncooperative weather, dash it all.

During the first couple of years traveling the Continent and other marvelous locales with her first employer, Mrs. Wescott, Trinity had enjoyed herself immensely. For certain, at the onset, she'd been homesick for England, but orphaned and raised in a foundling home, Trinity had no one waiting for her or anyone who cared about her, other than a few friends from her time at Haven House and Academy for the Enrichment of Young women.

Mrs. Wescott provided Trinity, a girl of unimpressive origins, with an opportunity of a lifetime. While Mrs. Wescott had preferred frequenting traditional and popular tourist sites, Mrs. Peagilly was a whole other precocious and tenacious creature. Far more adventurous and less attached to creature comforts than Mrs. Wescott, Mrs. Peagilly *relished the unexpected and scintillating adventure.*

Those were her own words.

Once, the courageous woman had found a juvenile, four-foot python asleep on her cot.

"I had left the tent unfastened, you see," Mrs. Peagilly recounted. "And the poor thing found a cozy place to curl up and take a snooze away from the elements."

Poor thing?

Trinity doubted her response would've been as sympathetic as Mrs. Peagilly's.

No indeed.

No matter their size, snakes were unpleasant, scaly, clammy, slithery creatures.

Was slithery a word?

The shudder that rippled over her this time was *not* from the cold.

Trinity had despised snakes for as long as she could remember. An encounter with a hissing, three-foot grass snake while playing in the garden when she was five had sent her shrieking into the orphanage. It had been months before she entered the garden or walked in the grass again. To this day, she would not venture into grass taller than her ankles.

And yet, here Trinity was headed to Morocco, home to puff adders, horned vipers, cobras, and boas.

Yes, but that did not mean she needed to venture into the nasty creatures' habitats.

She put a gloved finger to the dimple in her chin. Mayhap she should acquire a pistol, or at the very least, a stout stick—a large, very stout stick.

A mélange of heady expectation and sensible wariness wrestled for dominance as she considered what experiences she might encounter with her new employer.

"We need to move the gangway soon, Cap'n, else we shall miss the tide."

Trinity half-turned toward the speaker, Thaddaeus Compton.

The second mate—a ruggedly handsome chap in his late thirties or early forties—clasped his hands behind him as he rocked back on his heels.

"It'll be tricky enough navigating the river with this pea soup fog," Mr. Compton said.

Scanning his keen gaze over the pier, Captain Breckett puffed out his pewter gray bewhiskered cheeks, then gave a stern nod.

"Wait five more minutes, Mr. Compton. Not a second more."

"Aye, Cap'n."

The *clip-clop, clip-clop* of a horse approaching captured Trinity's attention. The hackney lurched to a bumpy stop before the *Daunting Duchess*'s pier.

"At last." Relief riddled the captain's two clipped words. "I was not positive he would make it, and sailing without him would've put me in a"—he sent Trinity a covert glance—"deuced smelly kettle of fish."

So they *had* been waiting for a passenger.

A very tardy and mysterious passenger.

Whomever they were, they must be important, indeed, to cause the captain to tarry until the last minute—the last five minutes—that was.

"I do not know why you waited on the bloody blighter." Contempt for the inconsiderate passenger permeated Mr. Compton's tone. He swerved his deep brown-eyed gaze toward Trinity.

"Beg your pardon, Miss Ablethorne."

"'Tis of no consequence, Mr. Compton."

Trinity waved away his apology.

He knew as well as she did that she would hear much worse on the voyage. In fact, the captain's *kettle of fish* was no doubt for her benefit—to spare her tender sensibilities. The only way for women to avoid crude speech on a ship was to remain in their cabin with cotton stuffed in their ears, and that she had no intention of doing.

Snapping his timepiece shut with a portentous *click*, Captain Breckett glanced upward at the mainmast, where an agile young man clambered up the stout pole, and then to the foremast, where another sailor in a navy peacoat secured an encased lantern.

"Because, Mr. Compton," the captain said with a side-eyed glance and a subtle jerk of his chin toward the newcomer, "*he* is one of the ship's owners."

"I beg your pardon, sir." Mr. Compton dipped his square chin. "I meant no disrespect."

Trinity was quite certain he had meant exactly that.

The captain merely grunted, and the second officer wended his way to the foredeck.

To better observe the ramshackle vehicle below, Trinity pushed her hood back a few inches. Not wishing to appear a snoop or busybody but unable to contain her curiosity, she lowered her head and peeped through her eyelashes.

One of the owners, hmm?

Wasn't that interesting?

Then why the hired hack?

Something was not quite right.

A tall man jumped out, a bulging satchel in his gloved hand. Covered from head to toe in a dark cape, he sprinted effortlessly up the gangway. The instant he set foot on deck, the men responded to a silent signal from the captain and scrambled to detach the gangplank. A bell tolled, announcing the ship's imminent departure.

The mysterious man, his features hidden in the hood of his black cloak, gave Captain Breckett a terse nod. Though Trinity could not see his eyes, she was certain his attention veered to her for an instant just as the wind whipped off her hood.

He visibly stiffened, causing the captain to send her a speculative glance before the ship's owner disappeared below deck. He had not spoken a word.

Without a doubt, someone had prearranged the owner's arrival.

Why the clandestine nature and secretiveness?

The captain and the first officer, Jack Alderton, a Scot as short and squat as Mr. Compton was tall and lithe, shouted orders. Men scurried hither and yon, and Trinity tapped her forefinger to her mouth as the *Daunting Duchess* slipped from her moorage.

Who was the enigmatic passenger, possessing power enough to delay the ship's sailing?

There were so many possibilities.

Did he even sail under his real name?

Probably not.

Which begged the question, why?

Well, Trinity had weeks to find out.

She always enjoyed a good puzzle.

As she pulled her hood over her head once more, she recalled his sudden rigidness when he'd seen her.

Did that mean he recognized her?

Now there was an interesting notion because, other than a single house party when she had first returned to England and tea on one occasion at Dr. and Joy Morrisette's, Trinity had not been anywhere other than services at St. George's with Mrs. Templemore.

Somehow, the latter seemed the least likely of the trio.

That left the tea and house party.

No, that left the house party. An intimate affair, the tea had consisted of a few close friends. This furtive fellow had not been amongst them.

Though tempted to follow the mysterious stranger below, Trinity resisted. He was not going anywhere, and she would not deprive herself of this last glimpse of England. Besides, what would she do?

Linger outside his cabin like a demented ninny?

A grin teased the corners of her mouth as she rested her elbows on the ship's rail.

What might've proved a rather unexceptional voyage had become decidedly more intriguing.

I hope you enjoyed this free preview of
LADY TEMPTS A ROGUE
Secrets of Scandalous Ladies
Book Six

If you'd like to keep reading, please scan the QR code.

©BLUE ROSE ROMANCE®

Thank you for reading NEVER A PROPER LADY. While this story is a sweet Regency romance with inspirational overtones, I also attempted to tastefully introduce romantic elements and sexual tension.

Enemies to lovers is one of my favorite romance tropes, along with marriages of convenience, class difference, and second chances and forbidden romance. NEVER A PROPER LADY contains elements of all of these, but Constantine and Faith and their budding romance make the story shine. My books are always character-driven, and often, while writing, my heroes and heroines persuade me to change the story to suit them.

Constantine and Faith are no exception.

I gave you a few hints regarding the next books in the series. The SIXTH book in my Secrets of Scandalous Ladies series is LADY TEMPTS A ROGUE. As you might have guessed already, that story features Trinity Ablethorne. I'm keeping her sweetheart a secret because while writing NEVER A PROPER LADY, an idea that changed Trinity's story popped into my head.

There are secondary characters in NEVER A PROPER LADY who have their own historical romances. These are their books if you are interested in reading them:

Mercy and Lord Ronan Brockman – NO LADY FOR THE LORD

Aston Terramier – LOVE LESSONS FOR A LADY

Joy Morrisette – A LADY'S SCANDALOUS WISH

Purity Mayfield and Theran Rutland – HIS ONE AND ONLY LADY

My next wicked earls' book, EARL OF RENSHAW, is also tied to the Secrets of Scandalous Ladies series. It features Sandford Brockman, Earl of Renshaw, the stuffy eldest brother of Ronan Brockman.

I have another important point I'd like to briefly touch on. Recently, a reader outside the United States became upset that I used American spellings in my Secrets of Scandalous Ladies Series, which is set in Regency England.

I use American spelling in all of my Regency and Highlander series.

Multiple factors influence an author deciding which spellings to use for their books. I chose American spelling simply because most of my reading audience is American, and my books are published in America. While I stick to a few British rules, such as *I shall* and *I shan't*, instead of I will and won't, I haven't extensively adopted other British grammatical rules and spelling. I believe my readers are flexible enough to adapt to slightly different spellings.

After all, it's the romance novel that matters, right?

To stay abreast of the releases of the other books in the Secrets of Scandalous Ladies series or my upcoming Chronicles of the Westbrook Brides series and new editions to the Wicked Earls' Club, and other books, subscribe to my newsletter or visit my author world at collettecameron-books.com.

If you liked Constantine and Faith's story, please consider leaving a review. Reviews really do help authors.

Hugs,
Collette

If you haven't joined Collette's exclusive mailing list click on QR image to sign up! You'll get access to exclusive content, sneak peeks, contests, giveaways, and more...
(P.S. No spam!)

https://collettecameronbooks.com/freegift

Collette loves to hear from readers.
You can contact her via her website: collettecameronbooks.com.
Or email her directly at collette@collettecameronbooks.com.

You can also follow Collette on social media:
Facebook: https://www.-facebook.com/ColletteCameronNovels/
Instagram: https://instagram.com/collettecameronauthor/
Goodreads: https://www.goodreads.com/collettecameron
Book Bub: https://www.bookbub.com/authors/collette-cameron

Pinterest: http://www.pinterest.com/colletteauthor/
YouTube: https://www.youtube.com/@ColletteCameron-
nAuthor

Giggles are Guaranteed
Collette's Cheris Reader Group

https://www.facebook.com/groups/CollettesCheris/

If you love to chat about all things romance-book related and enjoy taking part in fun and engaging live events, contests, and giveaways join **Collette's Chèris VIP Reader Group, https://www.facebook.com/groups/CollettesCheris/,** my exclusive private book group on Facebook.

Giggles are guaranteed!

Hope to see you there,
Collette Cameron®

ABOUT THE AUTHOR

COLLETTE CAMERON®

USA Today Bestselling author Collette Cameron® is renowned for her captivating, humorous, and heartwarming Scottish and Regency historical romance novels. With over 65 published titles, over 1.6 million books sold around the world, and multiple writing awards to her credit, Collette is a well-known author in the world of historical romance.

Readers love her witty and relatable characters including daring rogues, dashing scoundrels, and the strong and spirited heroines who capture their hearts. From the rugged highlands to the refined drawing rooms of Regency England, Collette's novels will transport you to another time and place, where love and adventure are just a page away.

Collette's Sweet-to-Spicy Timeless Romances® are the perfect escape for readers looking for romantic escape, poignant inspiration, engaging humor, and entertaining stories.

Based in the Pacific Northwest, Collette is surrounded by the lush greenery and rainy skies that inspire her writing. She dreams of one day splitting her time between the Pacific Northwest and Scotland. In the meantime, she indulges in her love of all things cobalt blue, dachshunds, chocolate, and of course, crafting her next historical romance.

Blue Rose Romance® LLC
collette@collettecameronbooks.com
collettecameronbooks.com

The Wallflower's Wild Wager — Book 1

The Spinster's Secret Stake, Book 2

DUKES COME CALLING
A Sensual Marriage of Convenience
Regency Historical Romance

A Diamond for a Duke — Book 1

Only a Duke Would Dare — Book 2

A December with a Duke — Book 3

What Would a Duke Do? — Book 4

Wooed by a Wicked Duke — Book 5

Duchess of His Heart — Book 6

Never Dance with a Duke — Book 7

Wedding Her Christmas Duke — Book 8

The Debutante and the Duke — Book 9

Loved by a Dangerous Duke — Book 10

How to Win a Duke's Heart — Book 11

When a Duke Desires a Lass — Book 12

My Dearest Duke — Book 13

FOR THE LOVE OF AN EARL (Wicked Earls' Club)
A Humorous Aristocrat and Wallflower
Regency Romance Adventure

Earl of Wainthorpe — Book 1
Earl of Scarborough — Book 2
Earl of Keyworth — Book 3
Earl of Renshaw — Book 4

HEART OF A SCOT
A Passionate Enemies to Lovers
Scottish Highlander Historical Mystery
Romance Adventure

To Love a Highland Laird — Book 1
To Redeem a Highland Rogue — Book 2
To Seduce a Highland Scoundrel — Book 3
To Woo a Highland Warrior — Book 4
To Enchant a Highland Earl — Book 5
To Defy a Highland Duke — Book 6
To Marry a Highland Marauder — Book 7
To Bargain with a Highland Buccaneer — Book 8
A Christmas Kiss for the Highlander — Book 9

HIGHLAND HEATHER ROMANCING A SCOT: CASTLE BRIDES

A Passionate Enemies to Lovers Second Chance Scottish Highlander Mystery Romance

Heart of a Highlander — Prequel

The Viscount's Vow — Book 1

The Highlander's Heiress — Book 2

The Earl's Enticement — Book 3

Triumph and Treasure — Book 4

Virtue and Valor — Book 5

Heartbreak and Honor — Book

Scandal's Splendor — Book 7

Passion and Plunder — Book 8

Wishes and Wonder — Book 9

A Yuletide Highlander — Book 10

SECRETS OF SCANDALOUS LADIES

A Romantic Class Difference Forced Proximity Regency Romance with Aristocrats

A Lady's Scandalous Kiss — Book 1

No Lady for the Lord — Book 2

Love Lessons for a Lady — Book 3

His One and Only Lady — Book 4

Never a Proper Lady — Book 5

Lady Tempts a Rogue — Book 6

THE CULPEPPER MISSES
A Humorous Wallflower Family Saga
Regency Romantic Comedy

The Earl and the Spinster — Book 1

The Marquis and the Vixen — Book 2

The Lord and the Wallflower — Book 3

The Buccaneer and the Bluestocking — Book 4

The Lieutenant and the Lady — Book 5

THE HONORABLE ROGUES®
A Second Chance Redeemable Rogue
and Wallflower Regency Romance

A Kiss for a Rogue — Book 1

A Bride for a Rogue — Book 2